A
WINTER'S FLOOD

~~~~~~~~~~~~~~~~~~~~

The Novel

Carmel Lile

❧ Gable Lantern Press ❧

www.awintersflood.com

ISBN 978-0-9974207-2-2

*to All who helped
my sincere thanks*

This story is set during a flood that devastated the city of Louisville, Kentucky, in 1937.

Go to **www.awintersflood.com** for:

~ a **story map** with the story's locations

~ period **photograph**s of Louisville landmarks mentioned in the story

~ an extensive **timeline** of the flood with photographs

1

Christmas Day, December 25, 1936

The traffic on West Broadway pushed slowly downtown. For a holiday, and so early in the morning, an unexpected number of people were out and about. From the backseat of Hank's Ford, Miranda could sense his frustration, in particular with the rusted-out Model-T putt-putting in front of them.

"Hold tight!" he warned and, honking his horn, pulled his sedan around the older vehicle. Pressing hard on the accelerator, he barreled down the streetcar tracks, straight toward an oncoming trolley.

Miranda dug her pumps into the floorboard. She squeezed the hatbox in her lap. Beside her in the backseat, Ben stomped his foot on an imaginary pedal and flung his arm across the front of her chest.

The streetcar's brakes screeched. Its normally cheerful bell rang like a fire alarm. Miranda pushed into the upholstery, unable to pull her eyes from the mass of green steel and glass about to plow into them.

Hank jerked the steering wheel and whipped the Ford back into the right lane, miraculously clearing the front wheels of the

Model-T. The streetcar clattered by, its driver glaring out his window. Only the people on board heard the blistering words spewing from his mouth.

Ben dropped his arm and relaxed into the seat. Miranda tensed forward, her body reeling from the scare. She scanned the traffic ahead, in dread of spotting another vehicle Hank might feel he had to pass.

In the distance, Union Station's narrow sign jutted out high over the sidewalk. Hank raced toward the station, not slowing even when the clock in the tallest tower was close enough to read the time. He wrenched the Ford to the curb at the front entrance and, before the automobile came to a complete stop, snapped his head around to grin at them.

"Didn't I tell you we could make it? Next go-round though, try not to turn off the alarm and fall back to sleep."

Ben reached over the seat and shook his hand. "Appreciate the ride, buddy." He stuffed a wrapped gift back into the shopping bag it had fallen from and, with a firm hold on the bag's handles, climbed out of the Ford.

Miranda slid across the seat, cradling the hatbox full of pecan pies she'd baked especially for Ben's dad, and swung her legs out to the mercifully unmoving sidewalk. Her winter coat billowed in the wind, and she rested a gloved hand against the side of her new felt hat to keep it from flying away.

"Gotta run," Hank said. "Peachie's fixing pancakes, and Henry wants to build a bridge with the erector set Santa brought him. See you back here tonight. Merry Christmas!"

"Merry Christmas," said Miranda, trying to gain her balance. "And thank you," she added, though mostly she was grateful to be safely out of his automobile.

Hank tipped his cap. With a negligible glance at the traffic, he gunned the motor and did a U-turn across three lanes of Broadway.

~ ~ ~

She hurried toward the limestone steps of the station, her legs unsteady. Ben reached the door to the vestibule first, holding it for her as he removed his fedora. When he pulled open the next door, which led into the concourse, a noisy confusion spilled out over them.

Miranda's step faltered. Something warned her not to go in. Ben eyed her curiously but, before he could say anything, she walked through the doorway and stepped to one side of the room.

Hundreds of voices, from far more people than she'd ever seen in Union Station, combined to make a terrible din. The holiday travelers juggled luggage and packages, bought newspapers and candy. Some prepared to board the trains leaving Louisville, and others, having just arrived in the city, greeted family and friends.

The noise of it all surrounded her and pressed on her, pierced her skin and reverberated through her body. She raised her eyes to the mezzanine, and then to the barrel ceiling high overhead, seeking some relief. A promise of outdoors beckoned through the skylights.

Maybe there was still time to go back outside and walk the perimeter of the station to the trains. Anything to keep from getting into the crowd that covered the length of the tile floor.

"Attention, please. Louisville and Nashville number twenty-three to Corbin, departing at eight o'clock, now boarding on track four."

Ben's hand pressed lightly against the small of her back. "That's us," he said. His hazel eyes, more gold this morning than green, shone with an eagerness to board the train that would take them to his parents' farm. The commotion did nothing but bounce off him. She found it hard not to envy his composure.

Her breathing uneasy, she wove through the crowd as quickly as good manners allowed, grateful for the employee passes in Ben's wallet that kept them from having to stop at a ticket window. Stretching her neck, she kept the rear doors in sight as best she could.

When they reached the rows of benches at the back of the station, where dozens of people sat waiting for their train to be called, her grip on the hatbox and her pocketbook loosened. Their last steps took them out the rear doors and into the cold air that swept under the train shed.

~~~

The brass bell atop a locomotive rang out a warning as a string of passenger cars backed onto a track under the train shed. Brakes squealed, and then hissed, as the train came to a stop. Miranda fled down the platform and away from the noise, turning at track four and boarding a day coach.

Ben came up the aisle behind her. He reached easily above a pair of empty seats, setting his hat and her pies on the overhead rack. Knowing she preferred the aisle seat, he sat by the window and put the shopping bag on the floor between them. She settled into the cushioned seat beside him and tugged off her gloves, dismayed to find her fingers trembling. She hated being nervous.

A stream of passengers followed them onto the coach, filling it from one end to the other until there were no more empty seats. Parents gathered children into their laps to make room.

Miranda stiffened with each seat taken. How could there possibly be enough air for them all to breathe? The only thing worse than being in the middle of a crowd was being confined with so many strangers. What if she had a spell?

Two shrill whistles traversed the closed windows, and the train pulled slowly from the station. No escape now. She was stuck the next hour and a half to New Haven, with nothing more on her stomach than the iced Christmas cookie and cup of coffee she'd gulped down at home.

She took off her felt hat, its sleek gray feather poking jauntily from the hatband, and placed it carefully on her lap, then leaned back against the white cloth that kept the seat's headrest clean. Out the window, brick business buildings, unlit and unoccupied for the day, came into view and disappeared again. She forced her fluttery eyelids closed.

She couldn't blame her nervousness *all* on Hank. She was the one who'd thought coffee might be a good idea instead of her usual mint tea. And it wasn't his fault so many people were traveling on Christmas Day, or that she'd had little sleep after her spat with Ben the night before.

Not a spat really. A disagreement. She opened her eyes and ran a finger across the initials engraved into the sterling silver bracelet he gave her after Midnight Mass. Right before the whole thing started.

She peeked sideways at him. Slouched in the seat, he held open a pocket-size manual on steam engines with both hands, his fair head bent over the compact pages. Absorbed by the text and tables, he seemed to have forgotten the night before.

The train left the city behind, rolling alongside stretches of harvested cornfields and winter-bare woods, landscape she usually found calming. But even a flurry of snowflakes, tumbling gently past, couldn't soothe her nerves.

After the stop at Shepherdsville, Ben's chin dipped to his chest. He slumped in the seat, his breathing slow and even. She slipped the manual from his hands before it fell to the floor. He was the one who should have had the strong coffee.

Across the aisle, a baby wiggled and squirmed in his mother's lap. Before long, his round face puckered, and his mouth widened into a cry that echoed throughout the coach. The mother, traveling alone with three children, all of them bunched into two seats, moved the baby up to her shoulder and patted his back. The screaming only escalated. Ben shifted, but he didn't waken.

The screams tore through Miranda. Was the baby hungry? Did he need changing? Was he sick? The wailing went on and on until she couldn't bear it any longer.

Her winter coat on top of her herringbone suit, which had felt good when she'd stepped outdoors at home, now all but smothered her. She unbuttoned the coat and half-stood to shake it off.

A wave of dizziness whirled in her head. She dropped back into the seat. Oh, no. Was she going to have a spell? Her chest did feel tight, and it *was* becoming harder to breathe.

The air pulsed with tension. Or was that her own imagining? She dug a handkerchief out of her pocketbook and wiped the perspiration from her hands. She couldn't have a spell in front of all these people.

Leaning out of her seat, she stared down the aisle at the women's lavatory at the far end of the coach. If a spell came on, she'd go there, where no one could see her. The thought soothed her, and she didn't feel as compelled to leave her seat.

The baby's crying let up, and she relaxed a bit more. Maybe she wouldn't have a spell after all.

The screaming started again. Miranda's shoulders drew up. She pulled at the back of her neck and kept an eye on the lavatory.

An elderly lady with a humpback rose from her seat, planted her cane in the walkway, and tottered down the aisle. Shrunken, fragile, and slow, the old woman took a long time reaching the end of the coach. She opened the lavatory door.

Miranda swept aside the hair that had fallen into her eyes. Now what? If she had a spell, there'd be nowhere to go, nowhere to get away. She crammed the handkerchief back into her pocketbook, crossed her legs, and uncrossed them.

She didn't know how much longer she could sit still. If she didn't get up, and if she didn't do it soon, her body was going to explode.

A drawn-out whistle signaled the stop at Lebanon Junction. A young man jumped to his feet and slung a string bag of oranges across his back. She shoved her hat onto her head and followed him out. Alone on the platform, she gulped in the cold air.

The conductor approached her. "This your stop, ma'am?" Plump snowflakes landed on his cap and the shoulders of his dark jacket.

"No. I... I needed some air."

He tugged on the gold chain dangling from his vest pocket and pulled out a watch. After noting the time, he turned his head and glanced toward the baggage car. Another trainman was rolling the car's steel door closed.

"Looks like we'll be leavin' straightaway." The conductor leaned forward, the bill of his cap nearly poking her. "You all right? You're lookin' a little pasty."

She took a step back. "I'm fine."

Shrugging, he headed toward the caboose. "Bo-o-o-oard!"

She forced her legs up the coach steps, her mouth dry. She didn't want to go back to her seat. Not while, no matter how many breaths she took, she couldn't get any air.

Her lips stuck to her teeth. She tried to swallow and couldn't. Tingling sensations crawled from her hands up her arms. Her vision blurred, and the edges of the train car darkened as if she'd entered a tunnel.

Panic rose like an eruption. She bolted down the aisle to the lavatory. *Please be open!* The door slid to one side. She stumbled in, locked the latch, and then sagged with her back against the door.

Her face, sickly pale against her dark hair, stared back from the mirror over the sink. Her hand flew to her hat. The gray feather was missing.

Darn!

Well, at least she was alone, and no one could see her.

The tension drained slowly from her body. She watched her legs shake, unable to make them stop. Her breathing came easier though, and she no longer felt she had to get away or die. Whatever had taken over her body was gone.

The door rattled as someone tried to come inside.

"Just a minute, please." The words, shaky and strained, sounded little like her own.

She straightened her hat and smoothed the tousled hair below it. With the last of her strength, she opened the door and walked gingerly to her seat, studying the floor so she wouldn't have to see if anyone was looking at her funny. The baby across the aisle sniffled in a fretful sleep.

Ben's head rested on the window. He snored softly. She sank down beside him, giving into the exhaustion and depression that always followed her spells.

She'd been right the night before, even if it had started a fuss. When Ben brought up the idea of adoption, she'd told him she wasn't sure she was ready. Now she knew for certain. How could she take care of a baby when she couldn't even take care of herself?

~~~

His dad stood patiently on the platform outside the depot as the train pulled into New Haven and they got off. Taking Ben's outstretched hand, he clasped it between both of his own. "Merry Christmas, you two." He patted Miranda's arm.

She impulsively moved the hatbox to one side and stretched up to kiss his shaven cheek. The whiff of crisply ironed white shirt beneath his denim overalls and the smell of outdoors ingrained in his jacket was the best breath she'd taken all day.

They climbed into the cab of Mr. Kinley's farm truck and headed out of town. The flurries had ceased, and the remaining snowflakes clung to the shriveled weeds on the side of the dirt road. Mr. Kinley kept the truck square in the middle of the road, only climbing out of the frozen ruts and moving to the right when another vehicle approached from the opposite direction. As he drove, he gave an accounting of everyone who'd arrived so far. Miranda patted Ben's knee with an unexpected contentment.

They turned into the narrow lane that led to the two-story clapboard farmhouse where Ben had grown up, following it a quarter mile and stopping near the back porch. No sooner had they gotten out of the truck than his five-year-old niece burst through the kitchen door and ran toward him. He handed the shopping bag to his dad and lifted her, spinning, in the air. Her squeals swirled around the yard.

Ben's sister scolded from the doorway. "Get back in here! You'll catch your death without a coat!"

Her mind on her daughter, she missed her small son wiggling past and darting outside. Ben hoisted him up and carried the children into the house.

The kitchen, bustling with family who welcomed them warmly, smelled of roast turkey and cinnamon. Ben's sister took the box of pies, and his older brother took their coats.

Crisp bacon strips and crusty biscuits overflowed a china plate on the table. Mrs. Kinley had saved them a bite, as she always did, to get them through to Christmas dinner. She turned from the wood-burning range and gave a smile that said she'd been waiting all morning to see them.

"You made it."

She wiped her hands on her flowered apron and came over to give Miranda a hug. The warm, solid embrace soothed the ache Miranda had carried ever since she lost her own mother.

"Look what I found outside," said Ben. "A couple of urchins we can turn into gingerbread. Open up the oven so I can pop 'em in!"

"No! No!" Giggling wildly, the children squirmed to get out of his arms.

He took a step closer to the range. A chorus of shrieks rose from their cousins, watching from a safe distance.

Ben stopped. "Well... Okay. If you're sure you can be good." He set the children down easy, kissed the tops of their heads, and let them go.

Miranda steadied herself on the nearest kitchen chair.

~~~

They walked side-by-side across the snow-dusted fields that led to the woods behind the farmhouse. Ben moaned and rubbed his stomach.

15

"Darn. I'm not going to have room for a turkey sandwich before we leave."

"I wouldn't bet on it."

She smiled up at him, glad to see he'd had a good day, and wondered if Mrs. Kinley's family realized what a gift she gave them every time she cooked. Miranda never took the generous meals for granted. There'd been too many times she and her mother had been down to flour and lard in the cabinet, and Miranda made biscuits and gravy for supper.

Ben had certainly savored his Christmas dinner, from the giblet gravy poured lavishly onto cornbread dressing to two slices of pecan pie after the children opened their gifts – a happy confusion in the parlor he'd enjoyed as much as the meal. He had leaned forward on his chair, his face expectant, as the boys unwrapped the wooden boats he'd spent weeks carving at his workbench in the basement. She'd contributed the sails for the boats, sewn from scraps of cotton duck, and made doll quilts for the girls.

Moving about outdoors was a nice change after drying dishes then sitting at a board game too long. The countryside gave her a feeling of peace, and she sometimes yearned to live somewhere as secluded and calm. But she couldn't picture herself not living two doors from Peachie, or not having Slatterman's grocery store at the corner and St. Benedict's across the street.

Ben reached inside her coat pocket and took her hand. "You've been quiet today."

"Who could get a word in edgewise?" She squeezed his hand to let him know she was teasing. "I wasn't feeling well this morning. Eating helped." She didn't want to talk about her spell. Recounting it would only bring back the awful feelings.

She glanced up, afraid he might assume she'd been trying to decide whether to adopt. She had promised him the night before she'd think about it. Now that she had her answer, she didn't want him to ask before she figured out how to tell him.

She racked her brain for something – anything – to say to distract him.

"Guess what? I got to see inside Mr. Johnson's house last night."

"*Inside* his house? Were the walls papered in exotic flowers like you thought?"

She rolled her eyes at him. "I said, *for all I know*, his walls could be papered in exotic flowers. Besides, it was the kitchen."

"When was this?"

"You were upstairs getting ready for Mass. I'd put the pies on the table to cool and turned off the light when I heard a noise outside. I went back and looked out over the sink. It was Mr. Johnson, carrying a bag of garbage to the alley. But then the wind blew his side door open, and I could see in the kitchen."

"See anything interesting?" His voice reflected the flash of humor in his eyes.

She made a face at him. He wasn't as curious as she was about their strange neighbor.

"It wouldn't be interesting if it were anyone else, but since it was Mr. Johnson, yes. His table was completely covered in food. An extra large ham, a three-layer cake, and I don't know how many pies."

"It *is* Christmas," Ben reminded her.

"But Mr. Johnson? You really think he's having company? I've never seen anyone stop by, much less come and stay for the day."

"Hard to say. He's an odd one."

"That's nicer than the other neighbors put it."

"Mrs. Slatterman, you mean?"

"Mostly. But Hank has said some things too."

Ben didn't answer right away. "Hank doesn't have any patience with people who won't speak to anyone. Does Mrs. Slatterman have something in particular against him?"

"Besides the fact that he lives on the same block and doesn't shop at her grocery store? She told me she cornered him one day to ask if he'd do some wallpapering up in their living quarters. He said he had too many other jobs lined up. She didn't believe him, and now she has these crazy ideas about where he's going and what he's doing when he leaves every day in his truck."

"Like what?"

"One day she'll say she wouldn't be surprised if he plans to rob the new gold vault at Fort Knox. Another day she thinks he's going to kidnap, or already has, somebody famous or one of their children."

"That's pretty far-fetched, and I don't know where it's coming from. Mr. Johnson is a decent neighbor. He may keep to himself, but he takes better care of his house and yard than the rest of us."

"I'm not sure what to think. I just hate to see anybody alone all the time."

The toe of her shoe caught on a rock, and she stumbled. Ben pulled his hand from her coat pocket and caught her.

"We'd better get back," he said. "It's almost dark, and we need to head out for the station before long."

The station. All the anxious feelings from her spell on the train surged forward and threatened to take hold of her again.

~~~

Her dread grew with every mile they drove to the train station. By the time they said good-bye to Ben's dad and went inside, her heart pounded so hard in her chest, it scared her.

The station agent, a head shorter than Ben and thirty years his senior, came up and clapped him on the shoulder. "Still workin' on that promotion?"

Ben grinned at his old friend. "Business will have to pick up a heck of a lot more for any of us firemen to make engineer. No complaints. I was never so glad to shovel coal as when the railroad called me back to work."

The agent's head bobbed in agreement. "Things sure did get thin there for a while." He turned her way and winked. "Did I ever tell you 'bout the day this young'n' came to town with his momma and daddy and hung around pesterin' me till the train from Atlanta pulled in? The little rascal was up in the engine 'fore I could stop him. Seems like yesterday, and here he is workin' on them engines hisself. Won't be long, I'm willin' to bet, he'll be runnin' one."

She managed a smile, but all she could think about was the moment, growing closer by the second, when she had to step back on the train.

A long whistle sounded in the distance. The agent cocked an ear and checked his pocket watch. "There's your ride now."

The men shook hands, and she and Ben left the warmth of the station. Her fingers trembling, she brushed away a snowflake that flew in her face.

The northbound train approached like a huge, black dog panting. The steam engine huffed past the platform, and the train stopped with a piercing squeal so loud she wanted to cover her ears. The conductor set down the steps and held his lantern to light the way.

Nothing to do but get on. She picked a pair of seats near the lavatory. The other passengers in the dimly lit coach dozed peacefully or gazed out the windows as if replete with memories of a good day.

The train rumbled through the dark countryside, blasting its whistle at every grade crossing and stopping in every small town. She sat tensely, wary of a spell, and urged the train forward. She wouldn't be able to relax until they were home.

When they rolled into Louisville, a Christmas snow, softly illuminated by the streetlights, brightened the sidewalks and streets. Falling thickly, the snowfall made it difficult to see as she and Ben stood in front of Union Station and watched for Hank's Ford to come up Broadway.

"Do you think he's forgotten us?"

"He'll be here soon," said Ben. "Why don't you go back inside, and I'll come get you."

"I'm fine. I like the fresh air."

But ten minutes later, covered in wet snow and her toes aching in only dress shoes and stockings, she considered waiting inside the door.

"Hold on," said Ben. "This looks like Hank now."

She wasn't sure how he could tell. All she could see were snowflakes glittering in the beams of two bright headlights. The Ford slid to a stop beside them, and Ben opened the back door.

"Sorry I'm late," said a voice that wasn't Hank's. "It took more than one I-mean-business threat to get my intoxicated husband to let me pick you up. Too much spiked eggnog."

"It's late, Peachie," said Ben. "We should have planned on catching a cab."

"I don't mind. Climb in out of that mess. You both look frozen."

Once they'd gotten settled in the back seat, she shifted into first gear and pulled smoothly away. The sedan skidded a few times on the way home, but she kept it under control and told them about all the fun Henry and Lucy had gotten into that day.

Miranda watched her and marveled. Peachie could handle anything.

2

A cardboard box, which once held cartons of cereal, sat inside the front door of the corner grocery store to corral wet umbrellas. Miranda wiggled hers in, splitting a soggy corner. She glanced up to see if Mrs. Slatterman had noticed.

Leaned over the counter on fleshy but capable arms, the grocery woman pored over the morning newspaper. Her black hair, graying at one temple, didn't dare escape from its tightly wound bun. She pushed the newspaper aside and acknowledged Miranda with a nod.

"Coming down buckets out there, ain't it?" Her deep, gravelly voice could send children with no business in the store scattering out the door. "Look at you. No more than three doors to walk down, and you're soaked."

"I'd have worn my boots if I'd known the sidewalk was going to be one big puddle." Miranda's brown oxfords, darkened by the rain, felt stiff and strange. There'd be orange patches on her socks when she took off her shoes back home. "At least the rain is better than last summer's drought. Someone dying every day from the heat," she shuddered to say it out loud, "and the ground so dry and cracked not even Mr. Johnson's garden would grow."

Mrs. Slatterman grew as still as the groceries lining the shelves behind her. Her eyes turned dark and menacing, reminiscent of the sky the afternoon a storm blew in and finally broke the heat. Her broad hand slapped the counter, startling Miranda like the first crash of thunder that had heralded the squall.

"Don't say that man's name in my presence!"

Miranda took a step back. Dropping her gaze, she fished in her coat pocket for the used envelope she'd written her grocery list on over breakfast. She handed the list to Mrs. Slatterman. The older woman pushed her glasses up her nose with a loud sniff and read down the list.

Miranda studied the downturned mouth. Why did one man's business matter? Slatterman's was large for a mom-and-pop grocery store. Besides serving the neighborhood, they delivered all over the West End. Not only had the store stayed in business through the worst of the depression years, but the Slattermans had given credit to their customers, she and Ben included, for as long as needed while jobs were scarce.

Ruth Anne, at work behind the candy counter, didn't seem bothered by her mother's outburst. Nor did one of the Harley's little boys, fidgeting in front of the wood and glass display while Ruth Anne opened a small bag and filled it with chocolate drops. Miranda was surprised to see the child buying the candy, since rumor had it his family could barely afford the rent on the shanty between Peachie's house and hers.

She and Ben weren't living on Osage when the man who bought the property next to them built a shanty on the back of his lot to live in until he could afford a bigger house at the front. He died before starting the house, and his wife remarried, renting the shanty to people like the Harleys who were down on their luck.

"Large coffee or small?" asked Mrs. Slatterman, her clipped words conveying she was still put out.

"Small." Miranda pulled her change purse from her other coat pocket and took out five dollars of Ben's pay. "I'd like to put this toward our bill while I'm here. Counting the last bit of sewing I did for you, our account should be up to date."

Mrs. Slatterman abandoned the grocery list and reached for the thick ledger at the end of the counter. She turned the pages to Ben and Miranda's account and recorded the payment in ink. Then she surprised Miranda by impaling her grocery list on a spindle.

"That's too much to be toting home by yourself in the rain. Junior is out on a delivery at the moment but, when he gets back, I'll have him box up your groceries and run them down to your back porch. Won't be more than an hour or so." She opened her cash drawer and added Miranda's money to a stack of rubber-banded dollar bills.

"You know, Ruth Anne is graduating this year, and she'll be needing one of those long, white dresses the girls wear." Mrs. Slatterman turned her full-figured girth toward the candy counter. "Apparently, the one Dolores wore four years ago won't do."

Miranda expected a look of annoyance on Mrs. Slatterman's face, but it softened as she watched her younger daughter give the Harley boy his change.

"Also, come May, Timmy needs a suit for his First Communion." She looked over her glasses at Miranda. "Do you think you can get those done for us? I know you don't have to, now that you're paid up, but the family has taken a liking to your sewing, and it's simpler than finding time to go shopping. Heaven knows I don't have a minute to sew, and Ruth Anne never took no sewing classes at school like you did."

Ruth Anne's eyes brightened, and she chimed in. "I want a dress with a skirt so full I can twirl around and make it swing out. Mother says all that fabric would cost too much."

"You don't need to be showing off your undergarments anyway."

"Mother!" Ruth Anne's eyes swept to the rear of the store to the man talking with Mr. Slatterman at the meat counter. Satisfied he hadn't heard, she turned back to Miranda. "What do you think, Mrs. Kinley?"

Miranda couldn't help herself. "I saw a pattern advertised in the newspaper the other day for a long dress with a cinched waist and full skirt. It was elegant. You would look beautiful in a dress like that."

"Humph," grunted Mrs. Slatterman. "Teaming up on me." She frowned at Ruth Anne, and then at Miranda. "You hoping to get more money?"

"No. I..." She squirmed under the woman's accusing stare.

~~~

Miranda stuck her umbrella out the grocery store door and thrust it open before she ventured into the pouring rain. Down the sidewalk a few steps, she slowed in front of Peachie's house.

There wasn't any need to go home right away, since Junior wouldn't show up with the groceries for another hour, and it would be nice to spend a few minutes with someone who didn't jump on everything she said. Besides, Ben was already there, helping Hank make a batch of beer.

She climbed Peachie's porch steps, rapped on the front door, and walked in. An overwhelming and off-putting smell of cooked grains shot up her nose. The beer-making was in full swing.

From the second floor, a more pleasant welcome drifted down. She strained to make out the words of the catchy tune Peachie was singing and recognized it as the song from the movie the four of them saw the previous Saturday. How in the world Peachie could memorize lyrics so easily, she had no idea.

Peachie skipped down the stairs, humming now. Her long waves of hair, as golden-red as a ripe Elberta, bounced around her slim shoulders. "Hello! Did you just get here?"

"A second ago."

"Come on back. The kids are in the kitchen, and the guys have moved their operations to the basement." On the way through the front room, she grabbed a tea towel from the arm of the davenport and ignored a dirty plate on the side table.

"What!"

Miranda stretched over Peachie's shoulder to see what had caused her to cry out. Lucy was crawling across the slide-out top of the Hoosier cabinet, reaching for the honey.

Miranda froze. "She's going to tip the cabinet on herself!"

Peachie raced across the kitchen and swept up Lucy. Her glare flew to and fastened on Henry, sitting at the table with a bowl of half-eaten oatmeal. "I asked you to watch your sister!"

He put down his spoon, innocence an ally on his offended face. "I did. She climbed real careful."

"Lordie." Peachie rolled her blue eyes toward heaven. She hid her laughter by burying a kiss on Lucy's cheek, their two heads of red curls merging.

Miranda returned the high chair Lucy had dragged to the cabinet to its spot at the table. Lucy might be petite for a just-turned three-year-old, but she didn't let that stop her.

Peachie plopped her firmly in the chair. "Finish your breakfast." She warmed her cup with a slosh of steaming coffee from the percolator and, after making sure Miranda didn't want anything, sat down. "What have you been up to this morning?"

"Grocery shopping." Miranda shared everything that happened at the store, from Mrs. Slatterman's temper down to the Harley boy buying chocolate drops.

Peachie giggled at the story about the graduation dress, but her smile faded at the last bit. "Did you hear about his little brother?"

"No. What?" The way Peachie asked made prickles of fear dance up and down Miranda's arms and legs.

"Potty!" Lucy reached wriggling fingers out to her mother.

"Hold on," Peachie said to Miranda and repeated the same to Lucy as she rushed her upstairs to the bathroom.

Wait! Tell me before you go, Miranda wanted to call after her. Instead, she carried Henry's empty bowl to the sink.

He was drawing in the sketch pad she and Ben gave him for Christmas – a fairly good depiction of a dog resembling Pepper, Father Donovan's mutt. The pencil clenched in Henry's hand had been whittled and sharpened to half its original size.

"Show me what else you've done," she said.

He flipped back a few pages. "This is Daddy's new Ford. And this is the Mu... Munipisal Bridge."

"Municipal." She praised each drawing, basic but surprisingly accurate, while her thoughts kept going back to the Harley boy.

Had he fallen out of a tree, the one the neighborhood kids always climbed, and needed stitches? Broken a leg? Or was it something worse like that child who'd had a pot of boiling water accidentally turned over on him?

A notion popped into her head that sent dread through every bone. What if he'd contracted polio? He was in first grade with Henry, closed up in the same classroom day after day. She studied Henry's face as he scrubbed a hole in the drawing paper in an attempt to fix the dog's tail.

"Does your head hurt?" She laid the back of her hand against his cheek.

"Nope."

"Are you feeling sick?"

"Nope."

"What's wrong?" asked Peachie.

Miranda drew her hand back self-consciously. She'd been so caught up in her thoughts she hadn't heard Peachie and Lucy come down the steps.

"I just got to worrying about the Harley boy. Does he have polio?"

"Polio? Why would you think that?"

"You sounded so ominous a few minutes ago. I figured whatever you were going to tell me had to be something terrible."

"Not *that* bad. He's selling magazines on a street corner over in Parkland. I know his family needs the money with Mr. Harley still out of work, but he's six years old. His brother is only seven, and I heard he's being sent to a relative out in the country this summer to work the farm. And, ten to one, that candy was for their mother, not the boys."

Hank came up from the basement, a cigarette dangling from his mouth, and rummaged through the utensil drawer in the Hoosier cabinet. "Whose mother?"

"Oh, nobody." Peachie shook her head as if to dismiss any more thoughts of the Harleys. She hummed a verse of the song from the movie and gave Henry an affectionate tug on his ear.

3

Sunday, January 10, 1937

Ben and Miranda arrived early for the nine-thirty Mass.
They took the end seats in the last pew by the exit, laid
their dripping umbrella on the floor, and let the kneeler down
to pray. She could relax now that they had seats where she
wouldn't feel confined.

Raindrops beat softly against the side windows, giving the
church a sheltered feel she found appealing. There was
something agreeable and unassuming about St. Benedict's, set
halfway below ground in the basement of the school building,
and she hoped the diocese wouldn't be in a hurry to construct a
large, separate church now that the economy was improving.

Because the parishioners at St. Benedict's, like the rest of the
city, were showing signs of getting back to normal. The ladies
wore hats more in keeping with the latest styles, and the men,
especially since Christmas, had on new neckties.

Most telling, though, were the soles of people's shoes, which
she couldn't help but notice when they knelt. Instead of large
holes on the bottoms of their shoes, with cardboard stuck
inside to protect socks and feet, more and more people had
new leather half-soles with fresh stitches sewn all around.

When Ben went back to the railroad, one of the first things they did was take his work boots to the shoemaker up the street.

He sat down, and she followed suit, her conscience nagging that she'd let her mind wander rather than say her prayers. But she couldn't concentrate on them, and she looked around to see who'd come in.

Hank and Henry sat toward the front. Peachie, who wasn't Catholic, hadn't been to Mass with them for a couple years, finding it less troublesome to stay home with Lucy rather than attempt to make her sit still.

Mrs. Broome knelt in the pew in front of Henry, her brimmed hat tipped to one side of her salt-and-pepper hair. Petite and neat and always busy with something, Father Donovan's housekeeper was another one for not sitting still long.

The Slatterman children took up a pew nearer the back. It was interesting to watch from week to week if Junior and Ruth Anne could keep the younger ones from misbehaving. Monday through Saturday, Mr. and Mrs. Slatterman rose long before the grocery store opened so he could drive downtown to the Haymarket and buy produce, poultry, and eggs from the local farmers. On Sundays, they woke early out of habit, and Mrs. Slatterman figured they might as well go to the six o'clock Mass. After she had the children out the door for the nine-thirty service, she and Mr. Slatterman enjoyed a leisurely breakfast.

The sacristy bell rang, stirring Miranda from her thoughts. Everyone stood. Father Donovan walked solemnly from the sacristy, the white and gold vestments he wore to celebrate the Feast of the Holy Family catching her eye. Two altar boys in black robes and white surplices accompanied him.

She opened her missal, searching for the proper page, when a movement behind her caused her to turn around. Mr. Johnson was coming down the basement steps. She'd never seen their next-door neighbor at nine-thirty Mass, and she had to stop herself from staring after him as he found a seat. A few minutes later, she glanced across the church. He sat in a pew close to the back rather than stand like the rest of the congregation.

The High Mass proceeded slowly – incense smoking, the choir singing, and Father chanting with enthusiasm. His sermon, a touching lesson on the Holy Family, was on the lengthy side, and she chided herself for thinking he might be enjoying the congregation as much as he would an audience.

At Communion time, Ben got into line with the other parishioners. He'd fasted since midnight, but she couldn't go without food and water that long and not be sick. She always felt conspicuous staying behind with the non-Catholic spouses and children who hadn't received their First Communion yet, half-worried people thought she must need to go to Confession. But she didn't want to risk having a spell in the long line or while kneeling at the Communion rail.

Not only because of the awful feelings that came with a spell, but because she was afraid she'd do something embarrassing like faint or, even worse, something crazy like run out. The less anyone saw of that, the better. Few knew about her nervous spells, and she wanted to keep it that way.

Mr. Johnson also stayed in his pew, and she wondered if that was usual for him. He'd had a cough throughout Mass, and he appeared to be swaying on the kneeler. Was *he* going to faint? She couldn't keep from staring this time and pleaded silently with him to sit down. He finally did.

The Mass ended, and she and Ben were the first up the steps and outside, opening the umbrella over their heads against the rain. They reached the street, ready to cross, when she realized that, in her hurry to leave before a crowd massed at the exit, she'd left her missal behind. They returned to the side door and waited for the rest of the parishioners to file out.

A few people had stayed behind in the church, lighting candles at the statues of the Blessed Mother and the Sacred

Heart or praying in the pews, rosaries in hand. Miranda picked up her missal.

Mr. Johnson was just leaving. He grabbed the pew in front of him to pull himself up. Halfway, he fell backward, collapsing into the seat.

"Look," she whispered to Ben. "I think Mr. Johnson is sick."

Their neighbor bent forward in the pew and held his head. Ben reached him first.

"Let me help you."

Mr. Johnson sat up and rubbed a meaty hand across the top of his balding head. His bushy mustache trembled, and he mouthed the first words he'd spoken to them the six years they'd lived next door. "No need."

Ben paid no attention. He put an arm across Mr. Johnson's back and both hands under his arms and lifted him from the pew. Miranda held out his hat, and Mr. Johnson fixed it shakily on his head.

As strong as Ben was from working at the railroad and helping his dad on the farm, he struggled to get the man, who could barely lift his feet, up the basement steps, and then outside and across the street. She held the umbrella over the two of them the best she could.

The last of the trek was mostly concrete steps – three up the knoll in his yard and a half-dozen at the porch – and took everything both men had. Mr. Johnson pulled a skeleton key from his coat pocket. With a wavering hand, he aimed unsuccessfully for the lock. Sighing, he handed the key to Miranda. She opened the door, and they walked into his sparse but spotless front room.

"Do you have a doctor?" asked Ben.

Their neighbor shook his head.

Ben turned to Miranda. "I'll get him to bed. Call Doctor Lathrop."

There wasn't a telephone in the hallway or bedroom. She tried the kitchen. Not everyone could afford a telephone, but surely Mr. Johnson needed one for his wallpapering business. The door to the only other room downstairs was closed, and she didn't think she could open it without feeling as if she were trespassing.

"I'll run over to our house and call."

~~~

She returned with a tin of tea leaves, a loaf of bread, and a dish of butter. Ben had Mr. Johnson in his pajamas and under the covers. His coat and clothes were draped across a padded armchair in the corner, and he appeared to be asleep. Ben followed her to the kitchen.

"Dr. Lathrop is at St. Mary's with another patient," she said, keeping her voice low. "Mrs. Lathrop said she'd telephone the hospital and get a message to him." She rubbed her hands up and down the arms of her coat. "Do you think it's cold in here?"

"I'll check on the furnace. Mr. Johnson must not have felt well enough this morning to load it. He's burning up with a fever."

While Ben was in the basement, she searched the cabinet drawers for matches and a strainer. With Mr. Johnson so bent on keeping everyone at a distance, going through his things, even in the kitchen, felt disrespectful.

She filled a saucepan with enough cold water to make tea for three. Ben preferred coffee and eggs, but he had to be hungry enough by this time to eat anything. She struck a match and lit the gas range then ran water over the burnt match at the sink.

Out the window, through the veil of rain, she considered her own house as Mr. Johnson must see it every day. How had he viewed her and Ben the years they'd lived next door? What had he thought? What must he think now, with the two of them in his house?

While the tea steeped, she made toast under the broiler, checking it every few seconds to make sure it wasn't getting too brown. When everything was ready, she carried a cup of tea and a plate of dry toast into Mr. Johnson's bedroom, placing them on the short chest by his bed.

"Mr. Johnson," she said, loud enough to wake him. She wasn't comfortable nudging his shoulder. "I've brought you some breakfast. It might help to eat a little something."

He shook his head without opening his eyes.

"I'll leave it then. In case you change your mind."

The house warmed up, and she and Ben took off their coats. Though it felt awkward and intrusive, they ate breakfast at Mr. Johnson's table and read his Sunday paper until the doctor arrived.

Dr. Lathrop closed the bedroom door behind him and stayed a good while with Mr. Johnson. When he was finished with his examination, he came into the kitchen, the curved lines above his bushy, white eyebrows deeper than usual.

"Influenza. Fairly rampant this time of year. I expect he'll recover with care. The problem is, he says he has no family or friends to help. He thinks he can take care of himself, but I know better. His only choice is the hospital, and he's refusing to go."

Miranda didn't blame him. She hadn't stepped foot in a hospital since her mother died. "Do you think we could take care of him?" she asked Ben.

"You wouldn't have to stay," said Dr. Lathrop. "Just check on him every few hours, make sure he drinks plenty of tea, take his temperature, and give him aspirin when he needs it. He'll eat when he's ready." He set his medical bag on the floor, its black leather edges faded from being jostled here and there. "Sure you want to take this on?"

"I'm willing if Miranda is," said Ben.

"Yes, I think we should," she said.

If Mr. Johnson took a turn for the worse, Ben or Peachie would be around. It wasn't the work – she just didn't cope well in emergencies by herself.

Dr. Lathrop buttoned his trench coat and pulled a checked cap over his snowy, thick hair. "See if you can find another blanket or two. We need to break that fever. I'll come by Tuesday to listen to his lungs again. Call if you need me before then."

4

Wednesday, January 13, 1937

She turned the knob and closed Mr. Johnson's front door as softly as she could, grimacing at the rainy mess her shoes left on the throw rug in his front room. After being out in the weather, even for the short time it took to rush down the sidewalk, she found his house, while not cozy and familiar like Peachie's, pleasantly dry and warm. She untied her wet headscarf and slipped it in her pocket.

She was relieved to find Mr. Johnson asleep, having learned early on it was easier to take care of his needs than carry on a conversation. When they did talk, each struggled to find something to say, and both chose their words with care.

The dishes from breakfast, which Ben brought earlier when he came to load the furnace, sat empty on the chest beside the bed. She'd sent farina with sugar, to build up Mr. Johnson's strength, but had left out the butter in case anything greasy might still turn his stomach.

An electric bill sat close to the edge of the bed, and a newspaper, *The Herald*, lay on the floor. They'd both come in the mail the day before, and she'd inadvertently learned two things when she'd brought them inside. Mr. Johnson's first name was Joe, and he had ties to Jasper, Indiana. Why else would someone have a small town newspaper mailed to them? She gathered the dishes off the chest and set the mail in their place, planning to add a note saying she would take his temperature when she brought lunch.

In the front room, she tugged on the heavy drapes at the window and let some daylight, gray though it was, into the room. Mr. Johnson's furniture was good quality, and his baseboards and corners were cleaner than her own. The room contained no adornments, extras a woman would have added. Several oil paintings did hang on the walls, unfamiliar landscapes too dark for her taste. Not a single wall in the front room, or in any of the rooms she'd seen, was papered.

The maple desk on the wall opposite his upholstered chair and table radio appeared the best place to find a pencil and paper. She moved toward it, experiencing the same qualms as on Sunday when she thought about opening the extra bedroom door. Surely it would be okay so she could leave a note.

The desk had a slanted front which, once she pulled it down, made a suitable place to write. Inside, at the top, a small drawer with a carved edge was fixed between two cubbyholes. One of the cubbyholes held No. 10 envelopes, the other a bottle of ink. When she opened the drawer, several pencils and a fountain pen rattled forward. Her breath caught at the noise, and she listened for Mr. Johnson to stir.

There was nothing he should care if she saw, only a few closed ledgers stashed beneath the cubbyholes and drawer. She took a pencil from the drawer and closed the top of the desk to check for paper in the bottom drawers, beginning to think it might be less embarrassing if she were caught rummaging through the garbage for a scrap of paper.

A fold-out map of Louisville was stored in the topmost drawer, with a sepia photograph and some sort of military service medal placed neatly on top. The bronze medal, with an angel bearing a shield and a sword, hung from a multi-colored ribbon with two silver stars. Mr. Johnson had been in the service? Maybe even the Great War?

A handful of manila envelopes and a stack of loose-leaf paper sat on each side of the map. She took the top piece of paper and folded a fourth of it to tear away, her eyes drawn to the sepia photograph.

The young couple in the snapshot smiled up at her. Dressed in light-colored traveling clothes, the two stood side-by-side on a trim lawn bordered with a profusion of flowers. Their eyes shone, and they appeared eager to be on their way. A honeymoon, perhaps?

The young man, his arm lightly but protectively around the girl's shoulder, had a face she knew. She imagined him older and heavier, added a mustache, and took away most of his dark hair. Was it really him? Stepping away from the desk, she carried the photograph to the window for better light. The young man had the same mole beside his nose as Mr. Johnson.

She turned the photograph over. *Jupp and Edda Geist, Jasper, Indiana, 1912* had been penciled painstakingly across the back. Edda must be deceased, because Mr. Johnson told Dr. Lathrop he had no family.

Why had Mr. Johnson changed his name? Because he was German? There'd been a good deal of anti-German sentiment during and after the war, but that didn't seem reason enough to be a recluse all these years later. Then she remembered what Mrs. Slatterman said about him being a kidnapper. Wasn't the man who kidnapped the Lindbergh baby German?

Oh, stop! It was she, not Mr. Johnson, who was doing something wrong. She glanced toward his bedroom, her face growing warm.

She placed the photograph back in the drawer, making sure it sat neatly on top of the map with the medal. She'd found out something new about Mr. Johnson, but her conscience wouldn't let her feel good about it.

~~~

Standing on Mr. Johnson's porch, dirty breakfast dishes in hand, she wished she'd brought her umbrella. Not because it was raining harder, but because the rain had slowed and Father Donovan had let Pepper outside. An umbrella might be some protection from the dog that had terrorized the neighborhood for years.

Pepper had quadrupled in size since the day he'd shown up at the rectory door, a scrawny short-legged pup tagging after a tramp who'd begged a sandwich. Miranda had watched from across the street that first day as Father Donovan pinched off a corner of the tramp's sandwich and tossed it to the pup. The tramp moved on, but the black-and-gray mutt hung around, and Father adopted him.

Still short but no longer scrawny, Pepper had a belly that nearly dragged the ground. He waddled now from bush to bush in the rectory front yard. Then he rambled down the sidewalk and past the school to do his real business in the yard beyond the convent. You wouldn't think he could move fast enough to hurt anyone, but mothers called their children home when he was outside.

He appeared to be far enough down the street for her to make it home without incident. She got as far as the sidewalk before an explosion of barks echoed through the neighborhood. Pepper's yaps grew louder and closer. She slowed her steps to avoid provoking an attack.

The barking let up, and she could sense him behind her. He sniffed her oxfords. His cold nose brushed the back of her leg. She flinched, nearly dropping the dishes.

"Pepper!" shouted Father Donovan. "Come here!"

Pepper turned and wandered leisurely across the street. By the time he reached the rectory, Miranda was inside her house, peeking out the curtains that covered the windowpanes on the front door. Father crouched in his doorway and rubbed the pesky scamp's ears. She couldn't understand the devotion, but Mrs. Slatterman said the dog gave the priest someone to love.

~ ~ ~

She spent most of the afternoon taking in school pants for Henry, who'd lost his baby fat that winter and had to depend on suspenders to keep his pants up. The floor lamp she'd positioned over the sewing machine cast more light on her work than the rainy day could offer and kept her from noticing the gathering darkness until Ben came in downstairs.

"I'm in the sewing room," she called.

He came up and poked his head in the doorway, his boyish smile brightening the shadowy room. "Supper smells good. How was your day?"

"Eventful."

"How's that?"

She stood, stretching, then walked over and kissed him. He leaned forward to keep his denim overalls, smeared with coal dust and grease, away from her dress.

"Why don't you take your bath, and I'll tell you while we eat."

On her way down to the kitchen, she paused on the landing and took the steps to the front room instead, where she switched on the lamps beside Ben's easy chair and her rocker. With Ben home and the lamps putting out a warm glow, the house cheered up considerably.

She was curious to see how he would react when she told him that their neighbor's real name wasn't Johnson. Would the news make him as suspicious as everyone else? The two men hadn't exactly become friends the past few days, but Mr. Johnson seemed to appreciate the help, and Ben was glad to do it.

When she took Mr. Johnson his lunch, she'd had trouble looking him in the eye. Not because of anything *he'd* done, but because she felt as if she had a sign hanging around her neck saying she'd been poking in his things.

Ben came downstairs smelling as clean as the bar of strong soap he'd used. She stopped stirring the pot of green beans and reached up to smooth a tuft of his dark blond hair, still damp from being washed.

"What's been going on?" he asked, after giving her a kiss he was slow to pull away from. "Mr. Johnson okay?"

"He seems to be getting better. He's still sleeping a lot."

She spooned the hot food she'd fixed onto their plates, and they sat down to supper. While Ben downed forkfuls of meatloaf, she admitted to taking the photograph of the young couple out of Mr. Johnson's desk. By the time she finished her story, her face had grown flushed again.

"It's a stretch to think of him married," Ben said. "A loner like him. Odd about his name too. It doesn't mean he's done anything wrong."

"Of course not." She was pleased to hear Ben defend Mr. Johnson. "I feel worse than ever for him, knowing he lost Edda."

The loss her mother endured came to mind. She hadn't become a recluse like Mr. Johnson, but her whole existence had changed when Miranda's dad died, and nothing in her or Miranda's life was ever the same again.

The glow the house had taken on when Ben came home suddenly dimmed. She put down her fork and told him about her encounter with Pepper.

"Has he ever bitten any of the kids in the neighborhood?" Ben asked.

"Not that I know of. But he scares them half to death."

Ben grew quiet after that, his head bent over his food until every bite was gone. He didn't tell her, as he did most evenings, about the freight they'd delivered that day or a prank one of the crew had pulled. Only later, when they were sitting in the front room, did he open up.

"We hauled a load from Belknap's up to Frankfort and Lexington today. You know the route, don't you? It runs past St. Joe's."

She had to think a minute. That wouldn't be the hospital. The church? "Oh, you mean the orphanage." Her stomach dropped.

"None of the kids were outside, but every window in the building was lit." The evening paper rustled in his hands. "There must be a lot of kids living there."

She put down the pair of Henry's pants she was hemming. Ben had let her go three weeks without giving him an answer. She shouldn't be surprised he was bringing it up now. "Yes, it's sad, but I would think the Sisters take good care of them."

"It's not the same as having parents."

"No. It's not."

"Have you thought anymore about it?" His voice grew hopeful. "Adopting?"

She picked a navy blue thread off her dress and rolled it between her fingers, studying the wisp of thread instead of looking at him. "I... I had a really bad spell on the train Christmas morning."

"A spell? Where was I?"

"You'd fallen asleep."

"You never said anything."

"I didn't want to talk about it." She still didn't. "But it made me realize..." She looked up.

"Realize what?"

"That I don't have what it takes to be a good mother."

"Miranda! You'd be a great mother. I know you would."

His voice held a plea unlike him, making her feel even worse. He hardly asked for anything. How could she tell him no?

"I don't see how I can do it," she said. "I'm sorry, but I just don't think I can."

The emotion drained from his face, and a pale mask fell in place. He leaned over, laid the newspaper on the floor, and rose heavily from his chair. "I'll go see if Mr. Johnson needs anything."

"Ben." She tried to convey in his name all the regret and anguish she felt. "I'm sorry."

"Don't worry. Forget I brought it up."

5

Friday, January 15, 1937

She scanned the sky from the front porch, hoping for a break in the clouds or some other indication the weather might improve. January was a bleak enough month without having to contend with all the rain. Today at least, it had slowed to a drizzle.

The doors of St. Benedict's burst open across the street, and the school children scattered home for lunch. The Slatterman kids, who knew better than to dawdle, headed straight for the grocery store. Henry took a less direct route, stomping in the puddles on the sidewalk and in the street and sending up sprays as high as his knees. Peachie was going to have a fit when she saw him but, after a long week of nothing but rain, the temptation was evidently more than a six-year-old could resist.

Miranda went down her wet steps and, unlike Henry, made an effort to avoid the pooling water on the sidewalk. By the time she passed Peachie's, he was inside and no doubt in trouble.

Next door at Slatterman's, the daily special was posted on the front window – canned salmon, the usual Friday fare. She pressed the thumb latch on the door handle and tried to recall if she'd used her last can. The bell above the door jingled a friendly hello. Overhead, the children scuffled across the second floor.

"We'll have it delivered by two," Mrs. Slatterman thundered into the telephone at the counter. "Plenty of time for supper." Her eyes widened when she saw Miranda. She cut her caller short and hung up.

"I have a bone to pick with you."

"What's that?" Miranda asked, not really wanting to know.

"When you were in here a couple days ago, you didn't tell me you were taking care of Mr. Johnson. I had to hear it from the ice man."

"It didn't seem that important."

"Is it true he's dying?"

"No. He was never that bad. As a matter of fact, he doesn't need us anymore, and I came to pick up a few groceries to hold him until he's strong enough to shop for himself."

"Well, it'll be the first time his groceries got bought here. He ain't having *you* pay, is he?"

"Of course not. He even wanted to give us something for our trouble this week, but we wouldn't let him."

"Probably dirty money anyhow." Mrs. Slatterman leaned closer and lowered her voice to the norm for most people. "What was the inside of his house like? See anything unusual?"

Miranda hesitated. She had no intention of giving away anything about the photograph, especially the part about the changed name. No telling where that might lead. "It looked much like anyone else's. Probably neater and cleaner than most."

"Humph. Is that so? I guess he ain't much of a conversationalist though."

"He slept most of the time." She handed over Mr. Johnson's grocery list.

Thankfully, Mrs. Slatterman's attention shifted to the list. She moved an empty box to the counter and filled it with boxes and cans from the shelves along the walls. Miranda escaped to the back of the store, skirting a pyramid of salmon cans and bushel baskets of potatoes and onions on her way to the meat counter.

Mrs. Broome, just finished at the meat counter, walked toward Miranda with a package likely containing a fish for supper at the rectory. Father Donovan's housekeeper nodded kindly and walked briskly past. She was always pleasant, but she never took time for much more than a hello when they crossed paths.

Behind the display case of meat and fish, Mr. Slatterman fed chunks of beef and fat into the grinder bolted to his work table. His slight frame belied his strength, and he cranked the handle effortlessly. Ground meat oozed into a large metal bowl. He stopped when he saw Miranda and wiped his hands down the front of his bloody apron.

"Good to see you, Miranda," he said. His brown eyes, always quietly amused, appeared larger than life behind the magnification of his eyeglasses. "What can I get you?"

"Sausages, please. About a pound's worth."

"Will do."

He pulled a string of fat sausages from the case and rested three on the tray of his large, white scale. "Been staying dry?"

"Mostly. You doing okay?"

He chuckled as he cut the sausages from the link and wrapped them in the square of paper he tore from a roller, and then chuckled again as he grabbed the pencil above his ear and jotted a price on the package.

"Fine and dandy as long as I stay out of trouble." He dipped his head toward the front counter and winked.

~~~

"WSM, Nashville. It's fourteen minutes and forty-seven seconds past two, Central Standard Time."

The radio announcer's words carried into the kitchen where Miranda was wringing out her mop. After three years of hearing the laundry soap commercial that followed, she could repeat it word for word. Deep, deep, deep, deep clean.

The only good thing to say about the overlong commercial was that she had time to carry the mop and bucket out to the back porch before her story started. She pitched the dirty wash water onto the rain-soaked yard and rested the rag mop against the house to dry. As dry as it would get anyhow.

Back inside, she curled up in Ben's easy chair, turned the knob on the table radio to a volume kinder to her ears, and snuggled under the afghan Mrs. Kinley had crocheted them for Christmas. The announcer brought the audience up to date on the week's story, and then dropped in on the mother, the show's main character, commiserating with her daughter over a failed romance. The family had a myriad of troubles, but at least it made for an interesting story each week.

"I don't understand," said the daughter. "I thought I was doing everything right. What's wrong with me?"

The girl's mother consoled her as the question echoed in Miranda's head. She shifted on the cushion and asked herself the same thing. What was wrong with her? Why did she have these spells? Why couldn't she be like everyone else?

Dr. Lathrop told her she wasn't the only person who had nervous spells. She'd never met anyone else, but maybe they tried to keep it a secret too. He also told her she was more sensitive than most people and advised her not to overdo it.

Then how could she ever adopt? You couldn't have a baby and not lose sleep. You couldn't have children and not need to take them places that might bring on a spell.

Over the years, she'd tried everything she could to get rid of the spells. She'd avoided packed and noisy places when she could and knew where to escape when she couldn't. She'd stayed at the edges of crowds. She sat by exits.

Ben had always been understanding – sitting in the back of theaters, taking the stairs instead of elevators, staying home the past New Year's Eve because she didn't feel up to getting in a crowd. But now that she'd told him she couldn't adopt, did he resent her spells? Did he hold it against her because he wouldn't have the family he wanted?

Sighing, she reached over and turned off the radio. The fifteen-minute program had ended and, not only had she missed the conclusion to the week's story, but she was no closer to helping herself than before.

~~~

Lucy, dressed for bed in her soft, yellow nightgown, was nestled in Peachie's lap. The two swayed with the music coming from the orchestra on the radio. Miranda, at the other end of Peachie's davenport, gathered a handful of buttery popcorn from the mixing bowl on the cushion between them. Any other Friday, such an evening would have been one of her favorite things to do.

But she couldn't get Ben off her mind. He had rushed in after work, cleaned up, and gulped down supper before flying back out the door so he and Hank could arrive at the Golden Gloves Tournament in time to get good seats. The evening before, the only other time they might have had a chance to talk, he'd come home late from a run to Maysville and gone right to sleep. She hadn't seen enough of him to figure out how upset he was with her.

"Did Ben seem okay to you when he came down?" she asked Peachie.

"His usual self. Why? What's up?"

"He asked me Christmas Eve if we could adopt. I told him I'd think about it, and then the other night I had to tell him I couldn't."

"Really? I've been thinking a while now you two might adopt." She'd known about Miranda's spells since high school and didn't show any surprise after hearing about the one on the train. "It does sound terrible, but are you sure you want to let it keep you from having a family?"

"Just because I want something doesn't mean it's a good idea." Miranda reached over and caressed Lucy's bare toes, the

47

skin soft and fresh after her bath. "I've always imagined myself with a daughter."

"Then why not do it?" Peachie rested her hand on Miranda's arm as if to siphon away any doubts.

"No. A child might be better off adopted than in an orphanage, but they wouldn't be better off with me."

"Oh, sweetie." Peachie rocked back and forth until Lucy's arms and legs went limp and her head dropped sideways. "I'll be right back," she whispered.

Miranda pulled herself up from the davenport and walked into the kitchen to look at the wall clock. Maybe there'd be time to talk to Ben after he got home from the boxing tournament. She could tell him again how sorry she was and how hard it was not to give him what he wanted.

Before he brought it up Christmas Eve night, she'd had no clue he wanted to adopt. Not that she hadn't thought about it herself, especially after Dr. Lathrop confirmed they might never have a child of their own. But by then, Ben had been laid off from the railroad for a year, and he didn't get called back for another two. Money had been scarce, with only odd jobs paying the bills, and it was all they could do to take care of themselves.

They'd done well not to get behind on their mortgage payments and lose everything Ben saved before they were married. While his buddies had used their paychecks to fix up automobiles or buy fishing boats, he'd put away his money for a house. A house too big for only the two of them.

The kitchen clock ticked the seconds, the steady clicking amplified by the evening's silence. She crossed to the back window and, bending toward the cold glass, cupped her hands around her eyes. Hundreds of stars speckled the night sky. The rain had finally ended.

Peachie came downstairs and brought the popcorn into the kitchen. "Now that Lucy's asleep, I'll let you beat me at a game of Gin Rummy." She pulled a deck of playing cards from the

Hoosier cabinet, along with a plate of fudge, and sat to deal them each a hand.

"Do you know what time Ben and Hank will be home?" Miranda asked.

"It better not be late. Henry's starting a cold, and he ought to be in bed." She laid a card face-up on the green linoleum tacked to the top of her ancient, hand-me-down table. "I'm still not sure how Hank talked me into letting Henry go. After the fights my parents used to get into, boxing is the last thing I want him enthused about. Hank knows how I feel about fighting."

Miranda drew a card from the deck and moved her other cards around to make the most of it. "You're lucky, you know. Being a good mother has come naturally to you."

"Some of it." Peachie broke into the smile that always warmed people to her. "For the rest, I ask myself what my mother would have done – and then I do the opposite."

6

Wednesday, January 20, 1937

"Now, ain't this sad?" Mrs. Slatterman scooted the morning paper across the grocery store counter and tapped sharply on a sizable photograph on the front page. "It's exactly what's going to happen to us all if this rain don't stop."

The picture had been hard enough for Miranda to look at during breakfast. A couple – the husband said to be eighty-two and his wife, fifty-six – sat huddled in the back of a city dump truck surrounded by the possessions they'd evacuated from their River Road home. They gazed down at their cast-iron stove, which reportedly still held a fire, keeping their eyes from the camera as if to preserve what privacy they had left.

"But they live along the river," Miranda said. "We're miles from the river."

"I'm just saying, it's gonna get worse before it gets any better. You've been out in that torrent today. Not to mention the creeks rushing into the river and more water flowing here from up east. We're not the only ones it's been pouring on."

Miranda's heart gave an odd thump. The constant barrage of rain did make her nervous and left her worrying where it would all end. Eleven days of rain, with Saturday being the only break. "I just need a couple things. A box of raisins—"

"Junior!" Mrs. Slatterman twisted around. "Turn that up before you leave!"

Her oldest son put down the box of groceries he was on his way out to deliver and walked over to the radio the Slattermans kept downstairs. A news reporter's voice rose in volume until it could be heard throughout the store.

"I don't want to miss President Roosevelt being sworn in," Mrs. Slatterman bellowed over the broadcast. "What he's done the past four years – and now starting a second term – it about makes up for all the bad news around here."

~~~

Henry lay on the davenport under a wool blanket shrunk accidentally to his size, his head sunk deep into a pillow propped at one end. Beneath his dark bangs, his eyes were puffy and bloodshot.

Miranda handed him a brown paper bag dotted with grease spots. "Maybe these will help you feel better."

He opened the bag and looked in but didn't reach for one of the oatmeal-raisin cookies. "Thank you," he mumbled.

"Your mother in the kitchen?"

He nodded glumly.

Peachie was folding laundry at the table. What smelled like ribs and sauerkraut simmered in a pot on the range, and Lucy lay sprawled across the floor, coloring on a grocery sack.

"What's new?" Peachie reached for a washrag to fold.

"Not much. Poor Henry's eyes look bad."

"He's still running a fever, and he's started a cough," Peachie's chin rose, "but his eyes look bad because he's been crying ever since I took *these* away from him." She lifted a pair of child-size leather boxing gloves from behind a stack of towels. "He evidently felt good enough this morning to hide in his bedroom and make believe he was a boxer. He thought he could close the door and keep Lucy out, and I wouldn't think something was up." She tilted her head sideways, and her eyebrows lifted. "Now who would you guess bought him these?"

"I hope Ben wasn't in on it."

"I'm sure it was every bit Hank. He's got Henry all worked up about boxing, and now I'm the bad guy. Not to mention that Henry knew to keep it from me. I don't know which makes me madder."

"I'm sorry." Miranda moved a doll from a chair and sat down. Hank was always one for a good time, no matter the cost. He'd had a reputation for being the neighborhood prankster when she and her parents moved next door to his family, though, to his credit, he was the only one who could get a smile out of her after her dad died. The problem was, he didn't stop to think how his antics might affect other people. Sometimes she wondered if introducing him to Peachie had been a mistake. Every time he did something irresponsible and upset Peachie, *she* was the one who felt guilty.

"Has Hank said how close the river is to the Ford plant?" she asked.

"It's getting closer every day. I hope they don't have to shut down. We can't make car payments if he's not working."

"Mrs. Slatterman is convinced that, if the rain doesn't stop, we'll have to evacuate."

"Oh, you know how she is, always thinking the worst."

"I just hate the idea of staying somewhere besides my own house." No telling where that man and woman in the city dump truck had been taken. "The newspaper said some of the people in the Portland neighborhood are living on their second floors. I'd rather do that. Move upstairs, and stay there till it's over."

"I'm sure we'll be fine."

The side door knob rattled, and the door swept open. Hank came in from work, his jacket dripping rain after only a short walk from his automobile at the curb.

Peachie flung one of his undershirts across the table. "Everyone except for my husband, that is."

7

Thursday, January 21, 1937

Miranda stared at the dark ceiling, uncertain what woke her. Waves of rain thrashed the front of the house, pressing like a threat. Was Mrs. Slatterman right in thinking the worst? Could the flooding actually reach them?

She shivered and reached for Ben. Her hand fell on his empty side of the bed. She'd forgotten for a moment he was working. Drawing the covers up to her chin, she huddled beneath them.

A loud creak in the direction of the stairs brought her up on one elbow. She fixed her eyes on the doorway, her heart racing. Another creak cut through the darkness, this one closer.

"Are you awake?" whispered Ben.

"You scared me half to death." She turned on the bedside lamp to see the clock beneath it. "Aren't you home early?" He'd left when she took Henry the cookies and said he wouldn't be back till nearly morning.

"We ran into flooded track all along the route and finally turned back. I thought about trying to telephone, but I didn't want to wake everybody on our party line."

"You're soaked! How did you get here from the railroad yard?"

"I hitched a couple rides and walked the rest of the way." His cheeks and hands looked painfully ruddy, even in the mellow light.

"Ben!"

He peeled off his wet overalls and unbuttoned his shirt. "I'll tell you more about it tomorrow." His voice fell off as he crossed the hall to the bathroom. "I'm too beat tonight."

She left the lamp on for him. Her heart took some time slowing to normal, and she was still awake when he came in from his bath, his elbow sticking through the tattered plaid of his flannel robe. The robe should have been sold to the rag man ages ago, but Ben wouldn't let it go.

He crawled into bed with the robe on, kissed her goodnight, and turned over. Within minutes, his back rose and fell in the rhythm of a restful sleep. She ran her hand across the washed-soft flannel covering his warm back, glad to have him home.

She would have liked to talk about a few things right away – what he knew about Henry's boxing gloves and just how bad the flooding was. Did she need to be worried or not?

There was no sense bringing up adoption again. The two times she tried, he told her he understood and asked would she please let it go. Afterward, both times, he had walked out of the room.

~~~

He came down the next morning closer to lunchtime than breakfast, tufts of hair sticking every which way on his head. She poured him a cup of coffee and slid *The Courier-Journal* across the table.

"The Weather Service is predicting the third worst flood in the city's history," she said.

"I can believe it. Beargrass Creek is spreading closer to the railroad yard every day."

She gave an anxious look out the window. "It's coming down harder today than it has yet. Do you think the flooding could reach our neighborhood?"

"As far as we are from the river? It doesn't seem likely. There's water in low spots all over the city, but that shouldn't affect us. Not with our house on a knoll."

"Mrs. Slatterman thinks we're in for it. Peachie thinks we'll be fine. I want to be prepared just in case."

"Prepared how? If it gets that bad, don't you think we ought to clear out of here?"

"I don't see why we'd have to." She didn't want to bring up her spells, considering the problem they were already causing, but no telling what kind of situation they'd end up in if they left home. Would it be something she could handle? "If we make sure we have plenty of food, we could stay upstairs till the water goes down."

"Let's not get ahead of ourselves. The only problem I've seen around here is that puddle on the basement floor."

~~~

The back-and-forth motion of Ben's handsaw sent grating noises up from the basement. He was making good progress on the cabinets he planned to hang down there. With the rain not letting up and the puddle growing, her mother's belongings, in boxes on the basement floor, might need to be moved into the cabinets sooner rather than later.

She turned on the radio, giving it a moment to warm up before she tuned the channel to something besides the farm report. When the broadcaster's voice came in clear enough to understand, he wasn't relaying the local hog and cattle prices she'd expected.

"...send you now to Shippingport where Mayor Neville Miller will speak. The mayor has just returned from the inauguration in Washington, D.C., to take personal charge of the flood situation."

The mayor, his tone professional yet compassionate, asked the citizens of Louisville to cooperate in caring for the refugees fleeing the area along the river just west of downtown. He spoke only a few minutes, and then the broadcast switched to a field crew across the river. Static crackled over the airwaves.

"...reporting from Jeffersonville, Indiana, for WHAS, radiophone of *The Courier-Journal* and *The Louisville Times*. The Ohio River, normally a half block's distance from the ten-foot-high levee protecting Jeffersonville, is inches from spilling over the top. Hundreds of workers are laboring feverishly to enlarge the levee, the only resource the town has to hold the river back.

"Word just in, L&N Railroad officials have announced..."

Miranda wavered between running to get Ben and staying by the radio so she wouldn't miss any of the announcement.

"...tracks flooded by Beargrass Creek, the Louisville to Lexington run will originate from the Baxter Avenue Station rather than Union Station. Beargrass Creek and its forks continue to spread far beyond their banks, flooding a portion of East Broadway and blocking the main traffic artery to the city's East End."

She darted to the basement door and called down the news but couldn't pull Ben from his work to come upstairs.

"Keep me updated," he said.

The reports and warnings continued through the afternoon, as did the heavy rain, which caused the river to rise faster than anticipated. She stayed beside the radio, for fear of missing something important, until Southern Bell Telephone and Telegraph reported more than 250 telephones out of order. She ran up to the telephone table under the window on the landing and lifted the receiver.

"Numb-ah, please," the operator drawled.

"I'm sorry. I was checking to see if we still had service."

She could feel the operator rolling her eyes.

Louisville Gas and Electric cautioned people to expect the worse concerning electric service. The Louisville Automobile Club advised motorists to stay home.

"Due to the extensive flooding, streetcars are limited, trains are running late, and Greyhound Bus service is paralyzed. At Bowman Field, the ground is saturated, making it difficult for heavy planes to land."

The city's Director of Health announced the establishment of two clinics where typhoid inoculations would be given to refugees. Miranda rubbed her arm. All the more reason not to become a refugee.

Garbage collection had been discontinued so the trucks could be used for relief work. She recoiled. They were hauling people in trucks that had held garbage?

Near the end of the afternoon, the Weather Service changed its prediction and warned that in three days the river would be nineteen feet above flood stage, making the flood the worst in Louisville's history. "The situation upstream is terribly bad," the meteorologist said, "and the prospect for Louisville can certainly be termed alarming."

Alarming. She couldn't sit still any longer. Maybe their house wouldn't be in the flooding, but there was a good chance they'd be without electricity. She went down to the basement to find the box from her mother's apartment marked *coal oil lamp*.

Ben glanced up from his work.

"I was thinking," she said, "if the electric goes out, we could use Mother's old lamp. Only we don't have any coal oil for it."

"I need hinges from the hardware store anyway." He set his hammer on the workbench. "If I leave now, I could make it to Parkland before they close. It wouldn't hurt to get more batteries for the flashlight either."

He brushed off the sawdust clinging to his clothes, and they went upstairs.

"Can you think of anything else?" he asked.

She lifted her hand to quiet him. "Listen."

"...evicted from their homes near the Cut-Off Bridge this morning and were taken to the Volunteers of America headquarters without furniture or extra clothing."

Evicted? The police could *make* you leave?

~ ~ ~

Darkness fell across the neighborhood. She'd been checking out the window for Ben over an hour with no sign of him. Pulling her cardigan close, she slipped out to the front porch and peered down the street. A cold, wet wind swept across the porch, whipping her hair around her face and raising goosebumps on her arms and legs. The glow from the streetlights revealed nothing but the slanting rain.

She picked up *The Louisville Times* from where the paperboy had landed it on the damp concrete. Her insides shook, and going back into the warm house didn't help. Unfolding the soggy newspaper, she laid the pages over the kitchen chairs to dry, and then perched by the radio on the arm of Ben's chair.

The flood news made her worry more, but she couldn't stop listening. Images of all that could go wrong ran like a movie in her head. *Flooded underpasses. Too dark to see. Automobiles careening off the road.*

If she wasn't afraid Ben might call while she was gone or that she'd put Hank in danger, she would have run down and asked him to drive around and look for Ben. She wished, not for the first time, that Peachie had a telephone.

Shivering, she went back to the kitchen and opened the oven door. The wafting heat warmed her hands, but the smell of the chicken pie she'd made for supper, its crust turning brown at the edges, turned her nervous stomach.

Masculine voices carried in from the back porch. She spun toward them. Under the porch light, Ben and Hank took off their coats and hung them on the hooks outside. She met them at the door.

"Where have you been? I've been worried sick."

"Sorry, hon. The store in Parkland was out of coal oil. Seems everyone had the same idea. I doubled back and walked over to 18th Street and found some there. Then I stopped to see if Hank had a minute to help me with the cabinets." He set the can of coal oil down on the linoleum floor.

She turned to Hank, her mind still on the flooding. "If our neighborhood floods, will you leave? Or stay with your house?"

Hank gave a lopsided grin. "That house is the landlord's worry. I'd load up Peachie and the kids and take them out to her mother's." He raised his fists up to his face then punched Ben on the arm. "That is, if Peachie will go anywhere with me. I'm still in the doghouse over that little boxing incident."

Miranda stole a glance at Ben. He had assured her he had nothing to do with it.

"She'll get over it," Hank went on. "It's Henry I feel bad for. He was fired up about his new boxing gloves, and now he's all down in the dumps. He's hardly been out of his room the last couple days."

"Aw, you know kids." Ben pulled batteries and hinges from his pants pocket. "Something else will come along, and it'll be forgotten by next week."

8

Friday, January 22, 1937

"Did you hear that?" Miranda propped up in bed and shook Ben's shoulder. "That pounding? There it is again. Someone's at the door!"

He sat up and reached for the pair of pants he'd left on the straight chair. She snatched her robe from the foot of the bed and fought with the fabric to get her arms in the sleeves.

The pounding grew louder and more insistent. They groped their way through the dark hallway and rushed down the stairs. Her head reeled from getting up too fast, and her stomach threatened to turn inside out.

Ben reached for the key by the radio while she pushed aside the curtains at the door. A tall silhouette, formed by the light of the street lamps, held open the screen door.

"Miranda! It's me!"

"Hank!"

She switched on a lamp while Ben unlocked and wrenched open the door. Hank ran past them, his wet shirt clinging to his lanky frame.

"I need to call Doc Lathrop!" He bounded to the landing in two leaps and picked up the receiver. "Hello! Hello!" He stopped yelling and turned to Miranda, his pale face blank. "The number!"

"Shawnee 2214."

He repeated Dr. Lathrop's telephone number to the operator. His wet hair, blacker than usual, fell to his forehead, and he impatiently shoved it back. "Come on, Doc. Pick up!" The relief on his face signaled the doctor's answer.

"Hank Ryan, Doc. It's Henry. He's hot as a firecracker. Coughing terrible all night, and now he's shaking like crazy. He's breathing fast, and he says his chest hurts." Hank paced across the small landing. "Yeah... Okay... Okay... Thanks, Doc." He slammed down the receiver. "He's meeting us at the hospital."

"What about Lucy?" Miranda asked, as he ran out of the house. "Do you want me to stay with her?"

"Yeah," he called from the porch steps without turning around.

"I'll come with you," Ben said to her. He looked as sick as she felt.

They threw shoes on their bare feet and coats over their nightclothes before racing down the sidewalk. Their feet plunged into puddles the night air had turned bitingly cold.

Hank carried Henry out of the house, his wool blanket wound around his limp body. Peachie held an umbrella over them, her eyes never leaving Henry.

"Hurry," she urged. "Hurry."

Ben beat them to the Ford and whisked open the passenger door. Peachie dropped into the seat and gathered Henry in her lap. He fought to breathe, and Miranda found herself struggling with him. She wanted to say something to Peachie but couldn't think what.

"I'll take good care of Lucy," she finally managed.

Peachie lifted her head. The cold fear in her eyes took what breath Miranda had left. Ben slammed the door closed, and Hank gunned the automobile down the street, his own door hanging open.

~~~

Miranda woke abruptly. The events of the night poured into her mind and settled heavily in her chest. She put a hand to the back of her neck and massaged the stiffness that had come from nodding off in the rocking chair beside Lucy's bed.

Lucy turned over in her single bed next to Henry's empty one, snuggling into the pillow instead of waking. Ben had gone home to be by the telephone. He must not have heard anything, or he would have come told her. As soon as Lucy was awake, they'd go wait with him for news from the hospital.

She got up from the rocker and tiptoed to the closet in the bathroom. After pulling a yellowed pillowcase from under a stack of washrags, she filled it with toys from the bedroom floor and clothes from a squeaky chest drawer.

"Mommy?"

"Morning, sweetie." Miranda eased onto the bed and brushed the curls from Lucy's face. "Mommy had to take Henry to the doctor. How about we go to my house and make egg bread? With brown sugar on top. Does that sound good?"

Lucy nodded, but her blue eyes, clouded with doubt, said she didn't quite understand. Miranda changed her into the print dress with the Peter Pan collar she'd made a few months before, pulled a pair of white socks up to her knees, and tied on leather shoes. Then she bundled her in the tweed coat and matching hat a friend of Peachie's had passed down and carried her out into the rain.

An automobile pulled up in front of Slatterman's, crammed with teenage girls sitting on each other's laps. Ruth Anne climbed out, laughing, and waved goodbye to her friends.

"Hello, Mrs. Kinley." She held a stack of school books over her head to protect the curls she must have pinned up the night before.

"Ruth Anne, would you tell your mother Mr. and Mrs. Ryan had to take Henry to the hospital last night? I'll let her know more when I hear." About to hurry off, she stopped. "Why are you out of school?"

"The river is coming up Market Street. Fortieth too. They sent us home!" She lowered the books and ran toward the grocery store. "Hope Henry's okay!"

At least someone could be lighthearted in the midst of all this. Miranda tightened her hold on the pillowcase, adjusted Lucy on her hip, and headed home.

Shawnee High School was seven or eight blocks from Fontaine Ferry, the amusement park alongside the river. She pictured the layout of the park and guessed that the Ohio River, which could be seen from the roller coaster, was normally a mile or so from the high school.

She never would have dreamt the river could overflow its banks a whole mile. The merry-go-round, the Hilarity Hall, the neighborhood homes outside the park – all must be underwater to some extent. If the river could flood that far, what would keep it from flooding another mile and reaching *their* neighborhood?

She turned up the driveway and went in through the back door. Ben was at the kitchen table with the back cover removed from the radio while he changed a tube. He got up and took Lucy from Miranda as if she were handing him no more than a pillow full of feathers.

"No word from Hank?" she asked.

"The telephone's been ringing all morning, but not for us."

She pulled Lucy's toys from the pillowcase and placed them on a chair within reach. "If the line's tied up, how's he going to get through?"

"When I was out looking for coal oil yesterday, all anyone talked about was the flood. I'd say, once they saw the morning paper, it only got worse."

The newspaper lay next to the radio. She leaned over the table and read the headline – "Record Flood May Cut Electricity in City."

"I rounded up our candles yesterday," she said, more bravely than the fluttering in her stomach warranted. "With the coal oil lamp ready to go now too, we should be fine."

"It's more serious than losing our lights," he answered. "The Waterside plant is weakening. The walls could crumble any time."

The Waterside plant. If that massive structure by the bridge could crumble, no wonder her whole life felt the same.

~~~

"Maybe we could call the hospital," she said to Ben, when he came up from the basement after working all morning to finish the cabinets. She was having trouble settling down to any real work, but he seemed glad to have something to do.

"It wouldn't do any good. You know the Sisters won't tell you anything unless you're family."

She set a bowl of tomato soup in front of him, along with a plate of crackers she'd smeared with peanut butter for him and Lucy, and poured them glasses of milk. She'd lost her own appetite. It was hard to eat or do anything pleasurable until she knew Henry would be okay.

She started a grocery list of canned goods and boxed cereal to have on hand in case the flooding got worse. After lunch, she tucked Lucy into bed in the extra bedroom and read her a book about cats and more cats so many times, Miranda was sure there'd be calicoes and tabbies prowling in and out of her dreams that night.

"Lucy's finally asleep," she told Ben, after tiptoeing downstairs. "I think I'll go to Slatterman's while she's down. When I get back, I'll empty Mother's boxes."

She'd rather sit and listen to the flood news but, after he'd worked so hard on the cabinets, it was only fair to get the boxes moved off the floor. She went to the pantry for her grocery money, kept hidden in a tea tin, before she left.

The rain had changed to a miserable sleet. A bitter wind pelted icy raindrops against her legs, stinging the bare skin between her coat and her socks. She was relieved to reach the inside of the warm, dry store and even glad, for a change, to see Mrs. Slatterman.

"What's this about our Henry being in the hospital? This ain't no time for more bad news. Things are crazy enough already – the telephone ringing non-stop with orders from people wanting to stock up, and Junior no sooner back from a round of deliveries than he's out again." She stopped and took a good look at Miranda, and the sharpness left her voice. "Tell me what's the matter with the poor mite."

"When..." Miranda fought down a rise of tears. "When they left for the hospital, Henry had a really high fever, and he had a hard time breathing." She was having trouble herself. "We're still waiting to hear something."

"Was he coughing?"

"Hank said terrible."

Mrs. Slatterman clucked and shook her head. "I don't hold to that old saying, no news is good news. If Henry was better, they would've had time to telephone.

"That's what I'm afraid of."

~~~

The heat flowing through the ductwork above her head kept the basement warm and comfortable. She picked up Ben's denim overalls off the floor and, one by one, put them in the wringer washer to agitate. His laundry couldn't wait until Monday. If the electric went off and she had to wash the sooty work clothes by hand, it would take hours.

She stood and watched the overalls swish back and forth in the hot water. The suds were grayish brown by the time she finally turned and walked over to the new cabinets and the boxes Ben had placed in front of them. She was in no hurry to go through her mother's belongings. Packing up the apartment had been hard enough. If the water on the floor hadn't threatened to ruin everything, she would have left the boxes in the corner untouched.

With the box marked *coal oil lamp* already open, she lifted the cardboard flap and carefully pulled out a weighty object swathed in newspaper. By feel alone, she knew it was the iridescent blue pitcher she and her mother found at a dime store on Fourth Street, the summer her dad moved the family from an apartment to their first house. Only seven at the time, Miranda clearly remembered the ride home on the streetcar. Her mother had called the pitcher "poor man's Tiffany" and laughed merrily. It was years before Miranda fully understood the remark and all her mother's reaction had meant.

After they arrived home and Miranda's dad had loyally admired the pitcher, her mother filled it with water from the kitchen tap and carried it out to a patch of hollyhocks near the clothesline. She cut and expertly arranged the stalks in the pitcher, and then carried her creation to a place of honor in the middle of the kitchen table. Late afternoon sunlight fell across the table and set off shimmers of purple and gold in the blue glass – just as Miranda's grandmother's real Tiffany must have done in St. Louis.

The pitcher had suffered a variety of chips over the years. She rubbed a finger across the rough top and set the pitcher on the basement steps to take upstairs.

The box also contained a pair of salt and pepper shakers, the *S* and *P* nearly rubbed off, and a teapot with a crack marring its glazed orange finish. Last, she found a pair of black-handled scissors. The dull blades sawed rather than cut the string off the next box, which held a bedside lamp and the dented shade that went with it. The lamp's cord was frayed.

She cut the string off all the cardboard boxes. Little of what she and Ben had packed up and brought home was usable. Except for the iron bed Lucy was napping in, the table and chairs in the dining room, and the sewing machine, everything of any value had been sold along with the house when her dad died.

There'd been no one to help them. Her mother's parents weren't the forgiving kind, and her mother wouldn't have asked anyway. She and Miranda took an apartment even smaller than the previous one. They shared the iron bed, and her mother found a job cutting fabric in the yard goods section of a department store in Parkland.

The one other thing her mother kept, because she couldn't bear to part with it, was the potbelly stove she and Miranda's dad had enjoyed sitting close to on cold winter evenings. Never used in the apartment, Ben and Hank had brought the stove down to the basement and stored it by his workbench. She studied the stove a minute then went upstairs.

"You know," she said to Ben, "if the flooding gets close, and we decide to stay, we could put Mother's stove in the bathroom and have heat on the second floor. There's plenty of space for it by the window, and it wouldn't hurt the tile floor."

"You're still thinking about that?"

"Well, you never know."

"We have Lucy to consider now. If the flooding reaches us, we need to get her somewhere safe. Maybe down to the farm."

"Lucy will be a lot safer here than out in this terrible weather. Besides, your parents don't have a telephone. Hank and Peachie might not be able to reach us."

"I don't know."

"You could pay Junior a little something to help you carry it upstairs."

Ben rubbed a hand across his unshaven cheek. "I could run a vent pipe through the roof, I suppose. Since the second floor's never as warm as the rest of the house, the extra heat would help at bath time."

"You'll do it then?"

"I could run down and see if Junior has a few minutes."

"And we don't have to evacuate?"

"I didn't say that." He had the decency to wink.

~ ~ ~

That evening the potbelly stove occupied a spot on the back wall of the bathroom, empty for the moment yet holding a promise of heat. Miranda dried Lucy after her bath, rubbing gently until her goose bumps went away. She pulled Lucy's yellow nightgown over her damp curls, helped her into a bulky sweater, and put thick socks on her small feet.

"There. Let's go downstairs and have some hot chocolate."

The telephone pealed two short rings, the first call for them all day. Surely it was Hank. Miranda picked up Lucy and ran out into the hall. Ben beat her to the landing.

"Hello."

"Any word on Henry?" The familiar voice on the other end carried beyond the receiver.

"Mrs. Slatterman. Hello. Let me give you to Miranda."

Miranda gave him an exasperated stare as she took the steps to the landing. With a grin not the least bit remorseful, he traded the telephone for Lucy and carried her down to the kitchen. At least Mrs. Slatterman was better than Hank with bad news.

"I reckon you forgot to let me know how Henry's doing."

"We still haven't heard anything."

"Not a thing? How can you stand it? It's been gnawing at me all day. I'd have to call the hospital and find out what's going on. Or go up there. Why ain't you–"

A brisk voice broke in that stopped even Mrs. Slatterman. "This is the operator. I have an emergency call for Shawnee 2365J. Would you please give up the line?"

"Yes!" Miranda unintentionally yelled at the operator. "I'll call you back," she said to Mrs. Slatterman and slammed down the receiver without saying good-bye.

"I think Hank's calling!"

"What?" said Ben. "How do you know?"

"The operator–"

The telephone gave a short ring. She didn't wait for the second one. "Hello?"

"It's Hank. I only have a minute."

She winced at the distress and exhaustion in his voice.

"It's pneumonia, and it's bad. The doc has Henry under an oxygen tent. Is Lucy okay?"

"I just gave her a bath. She's fine."

"Peachie will be glad to hear it. I'll call again when I can." He hung up.

She stared at the receiver. They'd waited all day, and it was over like that? There were so many things she wanted to ask, so many things she'd thought to say to Peachie.

Ben looked up from the string trick he was showing Lucy. Miranda shook her head. She couldn't repeat what Hank said without crying, and she didn't want to cry in front of Lucy.

9

Saturday, January 23, 1937

The harsh rings blasting from the telephone jarred the peace of the dark, sleeping house, repeating relentlessly as Ben tossed aside the covers. Miranda turned on the light and checked the time. Was it Hank? She didn't want to think why he might call so early.

Ben's end of the conversation carried up from the landing, but his yeses and okays didn't make clear who was on the other end. She hunted impatiently with her toes for her slippers on the floor and tightened the belt on her robe around the ache in her middle.

The light from the lamp spilled into the hall. She motioned to Ben to get his attention. "Hank?" she mouthed.

He gave a slight shake of his head. She took a grateful breath and, tapping a finger against her lips to get him to lower his voice, tiptoed into the extra bedroom.

Lucy slept on her side, her curls soft against the pillowcase. Miranda stood over the bed and soaked in the sweet sight of the small bundle curled in the woolen blanket. A sudden, deep yearning for a daughter of her own nearly swept away her resolve not to adopt.

Ben hung up the telephone. She expected him to come back up and tell her who had called, but his footsteps trailed farther downstairs. She started to follow him then noticed that, for not yet six o'clock on a winter morning, an unusual amount of light stole around the shades at the windows. She went to the front window, peeked out, and gasped.

Snow lay across the entire neighborhood. Broad expanses of white, brightened by the glow of the streetlights, covered the street, yards, and roofs. The transformation was stunning and, after days and days of dreary rain, the fresh, clean snow stirred a hope in her that things would change for the better.

The bed springs squeaked, and she turned back around.

"Mommy?" Lucy studied her surroundings with a pensive expression that wavered between curiosity and homesickness. Before she could think to miss Peachie too much, Miranda picked her up in the blanket, carried her to the window, and snapped open the shade.

"Look! Isn't the snow pretty?"

"Oh. Pretty." Lucy reached out and pressed her dainty hands against the window. The cold windowpanes, flecked with snowflakes, sent a chill up her arms.

Miranda tugged at the blanket to keep her warm. "Let's go see what Ben's doing."

They dressed and went down to the kitchen. Scraping noises from the coal shovel echoed up from the basement. She situated Lucy on the pile of books they'd stacked for her in a chair and pushed her up to the table. Ben came upstairs while she was filling the percolator at the sink.

"Would you mind fixing my breakfast while I get dressed?"

"Who was on the telephone?"

"The dispatcher."

"You're going to work?" The kitchen floor shifted beneath her. "With all the flooding, I thought business was at a standstill."

"They need me on a train that's carrying refugees to higher ground."

"What if Hank calls while you're gone? What if Henry...?" She couldn't finish.

"Don't think like that." Ben ran a hand through his short, sandy hair. "I don't want to refuse the work. The dispatcher swore I'd be home by evening."

She turned her back on him and walked into the pantry for eggs from the icebox. How could he leave with everything that was going on? She and Lucy needed him as much, if not more, than the railroad did.

When she came out, he took the eggs from her hand and pulled her into a hug that, any other time, made her feel cared for and protected. Was he really going to leave and let her deal with whatever happened on her own? She stayed stiff in his arms, not yielding to his touch.

"I wouldn't go if I didn't think you'd both be fine," he said quietly. "I'll be back before you know it. Probably by dark. If you need me before then, telephone the railroad yard. They'll get hold of me."

She pulled away, unconvinced.

After a quiet and hurried breakfast, he thrust his arms into his jacket and shoved his railroad cap on his head. She frowned at the insubstantial cap that wouldn't do anything to protect his ears. He gave her a kiss on the cheek and went out the back door. A rush of cold air swept into the house.

~~~

Lucy knelt on a kitchen chair while Miranda poured buttons from an old cookie tin onto the table in front of her. A few of the buttons were new, leftover from various sewing projects, but most were old, cut from clothes before they were sold to the rag man. Lucy reached for the biggest buttons, pulling them toward her with an interest that indicated she'd play awhile. Miranda took a sip of mint tea then untucked the morning paper and pressed it flat on the table.

Two bold headlines topped the front page. She couldn't remember seeing a double headline since the stock market crashed. The first warned of possible water rationing, and the second reported all oil stations closed. When she read on down the page, another story seemed far worse than the news chosen for the headlines.

Across the river in Indiana, the levee protecting Jeffersonville had given way the evening before. The Ohio River surged through the streets, covering the town with ten feet of floodwater. Cries of help guided rescuers, working in the dark, to people stranded on their roofs.

Her hand jerked, clattering her tea cup against the saucer. Only two streetcar lines were running in Louisville, both south from downtown. Ben hadn't been able to take a streetcar to work. With gasoline available only to rescue and medical workers, he may not have been able to hitch a ride either. Would he still be walking in the cold and snow?

Her unease made it hard to concentrate, and she skimmed through the rest of the newspaper. Nearly every story pertained to the flood. Governor Chandler had cut short a visit to Virginia to hurry back and direct statewide relief efforts. Louisville's Director of Welfare was opening canteens to serve refugees two meals a day.

She stopped and studied a map of Louisville. The map showed the areas, shaded in gray, that would be underwater if the river reached 52 feet. She flipped back to the front page where she'd seen, but couldn't remember, the current stage of the river – 48.5 feet. Finding the map again, she examined it more closely. Their neighborhood was in the danger zone, but in the corner farthest from the river.

The caption below the map warned that residents should be prepared to move if necessary. If necessary. She breathed easier. The precipitation had stopped entirely after the snow, and a fair day was predicted for Sunday. There was no reason to leave a dry and warm and well-stocked house.

A shout from the Harley's side of the house drew her eyes from the map. She scooted her chair back from the kitchen table and went to see what was going on outside the dining room window.

A pickup truck sat at the front curb, loaded with crates and boxes. Mr. Harley, in a heavy jacket but no rubber boots or hat, carried a ticking mattress to the truck along a path of dirty snow. Another man, struggling with a trunk, followed him. She presumed the man had brought the pickup truck. The boys came out the front door of the shanty next, their small hands clutching the scrunched-over tops of brown paper bags. They kicked at the snow and pushed at each other, finally making it to the truck. Were the Harleys running out on their rent or evacuating?

She moved to the front room window for a different view and looked up and down the street to see if anyone else was leaving. Mrs. Broome's automobile was parked in front of the convent, white steam billowing from the tailpipe while she waited in the driver's seat. Not unusual, since Father Donovan's housekeeper drove the Sisters wherever they needed to go. Maybe one of them had to see the doctor.

The school's principal, tall and lean in her black and white habit, came out of the convent. The other seven Sisters trailed behind, veiled heads down as they lifted their long skirts above the snow-covered sidewalk with one hand and carried a valise in the other.

About the time Miranda wondered how all eight Sisters would fit in one automobile, Junior pulled up in the delivery truck and parked in front of the school. He climbed out and opened the back doors. The Sisters placed their identical valises inside, and then divided themselves between the two vehicles. Miranda could only guess where they were headed. Another convent? The Motherhouse at Loretto?

She left the window and turned on the radio. Maybe WHAS had more up-to-the-minute news.

The radio station, broadcasting only flood news, made it clear that, except for relief work, the city was shut down. Catholic churches in unflooded areas would be open for prayer and Masses, with the heat and lights turned off to conserve utilities.

Water was definitely going to be rationed. The lines would be open from four to five that afternoon and again from eight to nine in the morning. She went back to the kitchen and tried the faucet. A few drips, and then nothing.

~~~

"You and Ben taking Lucy down to the farm?"

No *Hello*. No *This is Mrs. Slatterman*. Miranda had to take a moment and breathe after rushing to the telephone.

"Ben is working. We haven't made any definite plans to evacuate. Have you?"

"I ain't taking no chances with this flood, and there's no sense in keeping the store open 'cause we're pretty much sold out. What stock's left, we're carrying upstairs."

"Where will you go?"

"Up to Dolores's. That fancy house of hers has plenty of room to hold us. And she don't mind, I gotta give her that. She called this morning after seeing the map in the newspaper and insisted we come. Even our snooty son-in-law agreed. You and Ben need to take heed what that map says, what with having Lucy."

"I'm sure we'll talk about it when he comes home. By evening, he said. He's on a train moving refugees to high–"

"I can't hang on here talking. You need anything before we close up and take off?"

"We're good, I think."

"Mind you, you've got a big responsibility now, taking care of Lucy. If Henry kicks the bucket, she'll be all they have."

~~~

The overhead light lit up the kitchen as soon as Miranda flipped the switch. Maybe they wouldn't lose the electric after all.

When the water came on at four, running slow and smelling strongly of chlorine, she had filled the bathtub to the rim. She didn't want to scrape snow off the porch ledges and steps, as she had after lunch, to melt and boil for washing dishes. Chores already took longer than usual, having to keep an eye on Lucy.

With the neighborhood growing dark and less in the house to keep her mind off Ben, she worried how he would get home. Maybe someone from the railroad yard would be headed to the West End, or a rescue worker would pick him up and give him a ride.

The telephone rang, breaking the silence and startling her. Their party line, busy early on, had grown quiet over the day. She didn't know whether to hope the call was from Hank or Ben.

"Hey, hon." Ben sounded tired.

"Are you on your way home?"

"Not yet. Are you and Lucy okay?"

"We're fine. You're still at the railroad yard?"

"Yeah. It's been a long day, moving people from the yard to Spring Street. Beargrass Creek was halfway up the wheels, but we made it through. Back and forth, all day long."

"You sound tired."

"I'm feeling pretty rough."

"How will you get home? I saw in the paper the streetcars aren't running."

"I don't know. It's going to be harder now that it's dark."

"It's freezing too. I really don't like the idea of you walking home with no guarantee you'll catch a ride."

"I'll be okay." But he didn't sound happy about it himself. "Maybe, if you don't mind, I could sleep overnight in one of the cabooses that has a stove going. Once I've had some rest and it's light again, I shouldn't have any trouble getting home. Will you and Lucy be okay for the night?"

They would have to be. If she told him about the map in the newspaper, he might take his chances and come home no matter how tired he was.

"Get something to eat in the morning before you start back," she said. "Even on a Sunday, the canteens for the refugees should be open. Surely they're serving the workers too."

~~~

After supper, Hank telephoned to check on Lucy. Henry was no better. "I wasn't sure you'd answer," he said. "I heard everybody moved out of the West End today."

"Some of the neighbors left, but I saw a light on at the rectory, so Father Donovan is still here. Hard to tell if Mr. Johnson is home, with his drapes always drawn."

"You can't go by that old coot anyway. He's nothing but crazy. What does Ben say? Does he think you should evacuate?"

"He got called into work this morning. I wonder if we aren't safest here anyway. There's no sign of any real flooding, and I'd hate to take Lucy out in this weather."

"Peachie would probably agree. She doesn't know about the evacuations, and I'm planning to keep it that way."

"I'll keep an ear to the radio. If it sounds as if we're in any danger, I'll go across the street and ask Father Donovan for a ride somewhere safe."

"Okay."

"There's somebody here who wants to talk to you." She handed Lucy the telephone to say good-night.

After talking to Hank, Lucy cried for Peachie. Miranda quickly thought back to a song from her childhood and sang Lucy to sleep. A rather poor attempt, but it worked, and she took her up to bed. When she came back down, she listened to the flood news as she'd promised Hank. The radio kept her company as much as anything.

The Armory was filled with people from the West End who'd made their way downtown all day. The city had housed others in the upper floors of the Snead Building, and the Ohio

Theater was letting people come inside. How could you stay comfortably in a theater for any amount of time?

When the announcer reported that the Ohio River had all but stopped rising, she felt safe enough to turn off the radio and go upstairs. She slipped into the cold bed and, with only herself to warm the space under the covers, shivered a good while. Her mind raced from one thought to another. When it settled on Ben, and how everything would be fine when he came home in the morning, she drifted into the darkness of her exhaustion.

10

Rain pounded the porch roof outside Miranda's bedroom window. The din broke through her dreams, but her body, heavy with sleep, refused to move. A crash of thunder shook the house, forcing her awake. She turned on her back and listened to the storm that hadn't been in the forecast.

~~~

Reluctantly changing out of her warm nightgown, she shivered fiercely until she had put a cardigan over her dress and could rub the wool sleeves hard against her arms. With Ben not home, it would be up to her to load the furnace and get the house warm. She left the hall light off, so not to wake Lucy, and slipped quietly down the dark stairway.

The ceiling light in the kitchen cast only a partial path down the basement stairs. She went down the steps, holding onto the rail, then groped blindly for the light chain at the bottom and put a foot to the concrete floor. Cold water splashed onto her leg. She cried out and fled up to the light.

How much water had she stepped into? Two inches? Could all that come from a crack in the wall?

She stood a moment, paralyzed by not knowing what to do next. What she wanted to do was ladle water from the bathtub and fix a cup of hot tea. But it was freezing in the house, and it would stay that way if she didn't get some coal in the furnace. She found her rubber boots on the porch and the flashlight in the pantry and returned unwillingly to the basement.

The triangular beam of the flashlight skittered through the blackness. The water covered the caster wheels on the wringer washer and all she could see of the floor. She shined the flashlight on the furnace in the middle of the basement, its ductwork splayed out like spider legs, and splashed toward it.

She knew to open the air-flow first, and then the door to the firebox, where she banked the glowing remains and threw a shovelful of dry coal on top. The firebox provided some warmth but little light, and she was glad of the flashlight to illuminate the strangely sinister basement as she waited for the coal to catch fire.

Before long, blue flames rose and danced across the top of the coal bed. She shook down the ash, shoveling it into the ash can, then filled the firebox with as much coal as she could fit.

She waded to the steps. If the water stayed confined to the basement, they would be safe upstairs. They'd be warm only until the water reached the firebox.

~~~

Despite the heavy rain, the pale light of dawn stole into the house. Her fears lessened with the morning light and, as a pan of water heated on the gas range for tea, and another pan bubbled with oats, she went into the front room and raised a shade to keep an eye out for Ben.

The only person about was Mr. Johnson, huddled under an umbrella on his way to early Mass. His boots sloshed through the water in the street that the storm drain struggled to clear away. After disappearing beside the school building, he reappeared a few moments later and walked over and knocked on the rectory door.

She stayed by the window. It looked as if there might not be any Masses. In a way, that would be a relief. She wouldn't have to take Lucy out in the downpour and make her sit still for an hour in a cold church. But she was also disappointed, because she had planned to light a candle for Henry.

The porch light came on at the rectory, and Father Donovan opened the door. Pepper showed up at his feet and moseyed outside, ignoring the rain to venture down the steps and amble across the yard. Mr. Johnson nodded slowly as the priest spoke, and then turned and headed home. Maybe the church, being in the school basement, had water on its floor too.

Father shouted for Pepper, who'd made it through the water in the street and up to the sidewalk on her side. Apparently energized by his cold bath, the dog ran up Osage and didn't look back.

~~~

She didn't want to return to the basement anymore than she wanted to lose the use of her kitchen range but, on Thursday, Louisville Gas and Electric had warned customers to turn off the gas in any basement that was flooding. The possibility of an explosion, however exactly that would happen, terrified her and, the moment she remembered the warning, she became anxious to take care of it.

The water was higher on her boots than when she'd loaded the furnace. She slogged through, carefully at first to keep the water from splashing onto her legs, and then more hurriedly so she could finish and get back upstairs.

She'd never done anything with the gas meter except cautiously knock coal dust from it with a rag. She approached it as she might Pepper, her chest tight and pricked with pain.

The gas pipes ran from the meter at odd angles – one across the ceiling and up through the first floor, another in the direction of the water heater. The pipe that ran outside through the basement wall had a brass lever on one side. She could only hope it controlled the flow of gas. Circling her fingers around the cool brass, she took as deep a breath as she could manage, steadied her hand, and turned the lever clockwise.

Nothing exploded.

~~~

She searched the front porch for the Sunday newspaper. Their paperboy, a pitcher for a baseball team at Shawnee Park, never missed the porch and always had the paper delivered before breakfast, whatever the weather. Either his family had evacuated, or the newspaper offices were shut down along with every other business in town.

Father Donovan's automobile wasn't in its usual spot either. Was he out looking for Pepper? Or had he gone somewhere else to stay as the Sisters had? If he didn't come back, she couldn't keep her promise to Hank. Though, with Ben on his way, maybe it wouldn't matter so much.

She peered through the heavy downpour, wondering how long it would take him to get home. Hopefully, someone along the road had given him a ride. She hated to think how wet and cold he'd be if he had to walk the whole time.

Maybe, once he was dry and rested, he could find a way to vent the potbelly stove. The house was warming up, but she worried how long it would stay that way. And with no gas range to cook on, meals would consist of cereal and sandwiches until they had a fire.

Back inside, she crossed the front room and stopped at the bottom of the stairs to listen for Lucy. All was quiet, except for the rain, until an exclamation burst from her own lips. The coal they'd need for the stove was in the basement getting wet.

~~~

Patches of ice and snow, not yet melted by the pouring rain, crunched noisily under Miranda's boots. Though her winter coat shed the downpour, her headscarf was drenched by the time she reached the back of the yard. Raindrops rolled down her face.

She tilted the ash can she had fetched from the basement and flung the ash from the furnace across the rain-soaked alley. Setting the ash can aside, she dislodged her and Ben's trash can from the mud at the edge of the alley, turned its lid up on the ground, and dumped the garbage onto it. Her fingertips smarted from the cold metal, and she took a minute to curl them into her palms before carrying the empty cans back to the house.

She climbed the back porch steps, the trash can banging against the rail, and maneuvered the cans clumsily through the door. Once inside, both cans fell from her hands and crashed to the kitchen floor.

Lucy was on top of the table in her nightgown, crawling to reach the button tin. Miranda grabbed her from behind, blanching at the thought of the three-year-old, who didn't hold onto the handrail if she could get away with it, making a trip down the hardwood stairs alone. She seated Lucy on the stack of books, set a bowl of thick oatmeal in front of her, and promised the buttons for later.

Rain dripped from the saturated headscarf, trickling down her neck as she leaned over to take off her boots. She hung the scarf on a cabinet knob in the pantry, changed her coat for an apron, and found a rag to clean up the mud her boots had tracked across the floor.

With the kitchen back in order, she took the trash can upstairs to the bathroom and the ash can to the basement. Daylight seeped though the short windows at the top of the basement walls and lit her way to the coal room. The water nearly reached the top of her boots.

She shoveled coal into the ash can, and then lugged it upstairs, checking on Lucy before she climbed to the second floor and emptied the coal into the trash can. Trip after trip, from the bottom of the house to the top and back down again, she worked without stopping until the can in the bathroom brimmed with chunks of dark coal.

The final trip upstairs, she carried along what Ben would need to start a fire. Her legs wobbled on the way down, her quivery arms ached, and her feet, even in boots, were soaking wet. She sank into a kitchen chair and took a sip of tepid tea.

~~~

She knew that checking out the window every few minutes wouldn't bring Ben home any faster, but she couldn't help herself. Water spouted from the storm drain out front – much like the fountain at Victory Park where Peachie took Henry and Lucy to play – flooding the street to the top of the curb. Ben had to get home before it got any worse.

On the radio, the mayor pleaded with other cities to send police protection, typhoid serum, and food and clothing for the refugees. The river was rising again and wasn't expected to crest until Wednesday.

Somewhere outside, an engine turned over with a loud, cranking sound. Father Donovan came to mind, but his parking spot across the street was still empty. She walked in the direction of the revving motor and stopped at the pantry window to peer across the backyard.

Mr. Johnson was pulling away in the pick-up truck he used for his wallpapering business. He took off down the alley, not east, away from the flooding, but west toward 25th Street. Where could he be going?

She clung to the window frame. Mr. Johnson wasn't exactly a comfort to have around but, with him leaving, all her nearby neighbors were gone.

~~~

Lucy spilled buttons across the wood floor in the upstairs hallway, a good place to see her from where Miranda stood in the bathroom and contemplated the potbelly stove. Earlier, when she'd thought to bring Ben's tools upstairs and had gone to the basement to get them, the water covered the bottom two steps, too high over her boots to go down at all. It would reach the firebox before long, and they'd need another source of heat.

The potbelly stove had to be vented though, and the only way she could figure to do that, since she couldn't cut a hole through the ceiling or an outside wall, was to run the pipe out the window. Ben would know better how to do it, but she was afraid to wait for him.

He'd be in no condition anyhow. As long as it was taking him to get home, he had to be walking, which meant he'd be soaked through. The best place for him would be in bed under a pile of blankets. If she could have the upstairs warm for him, all the better.

The task didn't look that hard. She'd only have to break a small window pane. The stove's rusty vent pipe curved horizontally near the end and lined up close enough to one of the panes that she should be able to make it work.

She searched the sewing room for something to break the window and decided on her iron. After giving the undertaking a little more thought, she thumbed through a stack of fabric scraps and pulled out a piece of herringbone left from her Christmas suit.

She'd never broken a window in her life, and it took a minute, once she'd returned to the bathroom, to get up the nerve. With the wool held over the pane, she turned her head and hit the covered glass with the pointed end of the iron. Not hard enough. She squeezed her eyes shut and gave the window another blow, a good one this time. The muffled crash led to a tinkling of glass. Lucy stared at her from the hallway, more curious than concerned.

Most of the glass had fallen with the rain to the backyard far below. She cleaned up the slivers on the floor and pulled out the shards still stuck in the window frame. After some pushing and wiggling on her part, the round pipe fit through the rectangular hole. She tucked the wool around the pipe to fill the gaps in the corners.

If she was nervous about breaking a window, she was more so starting a fire in a stove that hadn't been used for years. She laid in coal and kindling then scrunched up sheets of newspaper to place on top. A match, struck against the grout in the tile floor, lit the balls of newspaper, transforming them into lacy, red orbs. Before long, the kindling and coal caught, and the fire grew. The flames leapt up at her. She hastily shut the cast-iron door and stepped back.

Outside the window, the smoke from the potbelly stove drifted gently away. The fire would soon warm the bathroom, and they wouldn't have to worry about being cold.

Why didn't that make her feel better?

~~~

The heavy rain and deserted neighborhood weren't all that had her jumping at every odd noise. The water in the street had risen over the curb and crept steadily now up the knoll. Where was Ben? He'd had plenty of time to make it home, even walking.

The man on the radio, his voice slow and precise, instructed rescuers listening at relief stations to send a boat to the addresses he relayed. In some cases, the people were ill. Other times, they needed supplies. But mostly, they wanted to be evacuated.

"Anyone below 15th Street must evacuate the area. If you live below 15th Street, it is imperative that you evacuate immediately."

She turned from the window and stared at the radio. They were ten blocks below 15th. Was that the first time for the announcement? She'd been busy feeding Lucy lunch then getting her settled on the rug with an assortment of toys and hadn't caught everything. Maybe Ben had heard about the evacuation. Maybe he hadn't come home because he assumed they'd be gone.

She folded her arms and pressed them against her middle, trying to staunch the rush of fear shooting to her fingers and toes. She couldn't do this without Ben. It was one thing, being stranded together. It was another, being alone and responsible for Lucy by herself.

Hank! Maybe she could telephone the hospital and get in touch with Hank. Maybe it wasn't too late to get an automobile through the water out front. She ran up to the landing and, with the telephone receiver to her ear, listened for the operator's voice. No one came on the line.

"Hello. Hello." She picked up the base of the telephone and sat on the stairs to wait. Her arms, still achy from moving the coal, quickly tired of holding the receiver. She switched it from ear to ear. The line stayed silent. The operators at the Shawnee Exchange must have fled to safety like everyone else.

She fidgeted on the hardwood steps a few more minutes, just in case, and then hung up. She could no longer reach anyone. Not Ben. Not Hank. Not even the radio station if she wanted a rescue boat.

Lucy threw a block across the rug. She pushed up from the floor and tottered toward the stairs, eyelids drooping and mouth in a pout. Miranda met her halfway. If she could do nothing else, she could get Lucy down for a nap.

~~~

Miranda pulled herself awake. Lucy slept untroubled in her lap, and the cat book they'd been reading had fallen to one side of Ben's easy chair. The warmth under the afghan must have lulled her to sleep, and she was tempted to drift off again and forget everything a few more minutes.

But things weren't right, and she woke more fully as each became apparent. The radio was dark and quiet. Water gurgled somewhere. The lamp was out. She stifled the *Oh, no* screaming in her throat.

Wriggling from under the afghan, she tucked it around Lucy and curled her into the cushion of the chair. The front room had a distinct chill. She bent down near the wall and felt the register in the floor. The metal was cool. The water in the basement had reached the firebox.

She could smell the dampness before she opened the basement door and took a few steps down. The wringer washer had flipped over in the rising water, and her mother's lamp shade was caught on one of its white legs. All Ben's hard work, and her mother's things hadn't stayed out of the water after all.

She snatched her boots from the top step and shut the door, sliding the deadbolt Ben had installed because he sometimes worked at night. If only the lock could keep out the floodwater as well as it could intruders.

When she'd first thought about staying home rather than evacuating, the second floor had seemed an impossible distance for the flood to reach. Now, with her stomach quivering in time with her heart, she wasn't so sure.

What worried her most though, if she didn't count Henry, was Ben. Where could he be? He knew how much she wanted to stay at the house. Even if he'd heard about the danger below 15th Street, he wouldn't assume she'd leave.

~~~

A loud thunk sent her running to the front door. Ben! She flung open the door. All that waited beyond the screen door was floodwater. The yard had disappeared, and the murky water taking over the neighborhood sloshed against the porch steps. St. Benedict's and all the houses on the street were islands. Empty, deserted islands. The rain poured relentlessly on the lot of them, washing away the last of her hope.

Something wooden groaned to her right. She pushed open the screen door and leaned out. Mr. Johnson was crawling across a ladder that ran from the side window of his front room to her porch.

"Mr. Johnson!" Her knees nearly gave way, and a shaky laugh bubbled up from her throat. Seeing her neighbor creep across a ladder was the last thing she'd expected.

Nimble for his weight and age, he had little trouble maneuvering himself off the ladder and onto the porch. Rain dripped off the cap above his florid face.

"Just came to see if you and Ben need anything," he said, his voice louder than what she'd been used to when he was sick.

"Would you like to come in?" There was too much to say to hang out the door and do it.

"Maybe for a minute."

He removed his cap and wiped his feet on the rug inside the door. An odd look came over his face when he noticed Lucy asleep in the chair.

"You and Ben have the Ryans' little girl."

"Well, I do. Ben got called into work yesterday. He was supposed to return home this morning. I don't know what's happened to him."

Lucy stretched her arms and legs against the chair and sat up.

"You're stranded here alone with the child?" said Mr. Johnson. "Without heat?"

"We have my mother's old coal stove."

His eyes searched the front room.

"It's upstairs." She motioned for him to have a seat on the davenport. "I saw you drive away in your truck a couple hours ago. I thought you were leaving."

He sat on the edge of the cushion as if he might bolt any moment. "When the water climbed over the curb, I decided to park my truck somewhere higher. I drove south on 26th until the streets weren't flooded and left it in the parking lot of an oil station on a rise. You must not have seen me walk home."

She grew warm, embarrassed that he assumed she was watching him. Looking down at her hands, she played with her wedding ring. "I've been pretty busy with Lucy. And moving food and stuff upstairs."

"You're going to stay here with the child then?"

"I planned on Ben being here too, but we do have everything we need."

Mr. Johnson's next words were subdued, and he spoke them gently. "What if she were to get sick? With something you couldn't take care of?"

"There's less risk of that if I don't take her out in this weather."

"What if it's something she's already been exposed to?" It seemed to pain him to go on. "I understand her brother is in the hospital and very ill."

"Yes. I didn't know you'd heard."

"Father Donovan told me this morning. He..." Mr. Johnson turned to look at Lucy. Her head had dropped to the arm of the chair, and she'd fallen back to sleep.

Miranda slipped her wedding band nervously up and down her finger, waiting for him to go on.

"He'd just received a telephone call from the hospital."

She could feel the color drain from her face and, afraid she'd faint, she stirred herself sharply.

"The Sisters asked him to come and give the boy Last Rites," said Mr. Johnson. "The Sunday Mass obligation was lifted by the bishop, and Father was getting ready to leave for the hospital."

The Last Rites. So that's where Father Donovan had gone. To St. Mary's. To give Henry the Last Rites. Her chest swelled until it ached. The Last Rites. A priest from Holy Cross had come to the hospital to give her mother Last Rites, a sacrament reserved for the dying. The tears Miranda had been holding back all afternoon blurred Mr. Johnson's face.

"Excuse me," she mumbled, jumping up and running into the kitchen before the tears escaped down her cheeks. She stopped at the sink, grabbing onto its edge, and heaved silent sobs. *Oh, Henry. Oh, Peachie.* Something reached inside her chest and squeezed until she felt she might die too.

Footsteps padded across the front room. Back and forth. Back and forth. Poor Mr. Johnson. He hadn't wanted to tell her about Henry. He hadn't wanted to pass on the terrible news.

A fresh wave of tears threatened. She took a shaky breath and swiped at her wet cheeks. Crying wasn't going to help anything.

~~~

"I'm not sure where Lucy and I would even go," said Miranda, after, at Mr. Johnson's suggestion, they carried the kitchen and dining room chairs upstairs.

He pulled a striped handkerchief from his jacket pocket and wiped off the perspiration dripping down his face. "No family in town?"

"My parents are dead, and their families are in St. Louis. They were estranged anyway." Why had she told him that? "Ben's parents have a farm down in New Haven, but I doubt a train could get through."

"What about the refugee centers in the East End? There'd be a doctor nearby."

"It's too late now. I can't get hold of anyone to take us."

Mr. Johnson's eyes, dark under heavy brows, grew distant as he stopped to think. "Before the electric went off, the radio said rescue boats would patrol the flooded areas. They said put a candle in the window, once it's dark, if you want them to stop."

"I haven't seen or heard any boats, have you?"

"Can't say I have."

"If one did come by, I could ask them to take us to St. Mary's. Lucy would have to stay in the parlor, of course, but Peachie could come down and see her."

And why had she said that? She had no desire to go to the hospital now that she knew Henry had been given the Last Rites. The thought of being there when he died stiffened her with the worst kind of dread and sorrow.

"That's not really a good idea," she added quickly. "We'd have no place to sleep, and Hank would have to leave Henry to take us somewhere else."

The relief she found in the excuse was short-lived. She was nothing but a coward. Henry was the real reason she didn't want to go to the hospital. If she could find it in herself to be brave, she might be of some comfort to Peachie.

Mr. Johnson didn't offer any thoughts on St. Mary's. "What about the furniture here in the front room?"

"The davenport is too bulky to carry up the steps, but we could take the radio and table."

When they came back down, Lucy was rousing again. Miranda sat on the arm of Ben's chair and smoothed a tendril of hair from her eyes. Did she look paler than usual? Was that sniff normal or a symptom of some impending illness?

If Lucy were to have as much trouble breathing as Henry the other night, Miranda would have no idea how to help her. How had she thought she could?

She'll be all they have. Who'd said that? She searched her weary mind. Mrs. Slatterman. On the telephone the day before. Miranda hadn't believed she could say such a thing, but it was painfully true.

Maybe Mr. Johnson and Mrs. Slatterman were right. Maybe she should take Lucy where she'd have the best care. And then maybe, just maybe, that would make up for being such a coward.

~~~

Mr. Johnson kept an eye on Lucy from the chair he'd situated between the hot surface of the potbelly stove and the spot where she was stretched out on the tile floor eating an apple butter sandwich and flipping through her cat book. On the chair beside him, the coal oil lamp cast flickers of light across the walls of the roomy bathroom. The short winter day had turned to dusk.

Miranda stood in the doorway, Lucy's clothes piled in her arms. "Will you go with us?"

He was quick to shake his head. "No reason to. I'm better off at home."

She wished she could say the same. Despite the threat of the rising floodwater, her second floor felt like a haven from the persistent rain and cold night.

"Would you want to stay here? You'd have heat, there's plenty of food and, if Ben makes it home, you could tell him where Lucy and I have gone."

"Appreciate the offer, but I'll head home once you're packed. Maybe you could leave Ben a note." His leg bounced incessantly.

"Of course. There's no sense in you staying any longer than that. Who knows when a boat will come along?"

She crossed the dim hallway to her bedroom. Rain pelted the roof, not quite drowning out the sound of the floodwater lapping against the house. The candle on the windowsill shined fitfully, as uncertain of its ability to stay lit as she felt about handling the days ahead.

She laid Lucy's clothes on the bed then knelt beside it to grope under the springs for the suitcase. Her fingers caught hold of the Bakelite handle, and she pulled out the gift Ben's parents had given them for their wedding. The small suitcase was perfect for a short stay at the farm, but it would be a tight fit for everything she and Lucy might need. At least she shouldn't have trouble carrying it.

Wisps of dust clung to the edges of the leather case. She brushed them onto the floor and laid the suitcase on the bedspread. Her thumbs twitched as she pushed on the locks. The latches flew open, and she lifted the lid.

The cloth lining inside released a fragrance of spilled shaving cream. She leaned forward, her eyelids slipping closed, and savored the scent that made Ben seem inches away. If only she could go back and rest her head against his chest, giving into the embrace she'd refused before he left.

She straightened with a sigh and went to the closet. With no light other than the candle on the opposite side of the room, the clothes hanging inside had little color or shape.

She ran her hands across the garments on her side of the closet. What should she take? Not the dress with the itchy collar. But definitely her warmest sweater.

She felt for the thick, cable-knit sweater and for the daytime dress with the tucks down the front she'd had for years. No sense taking the risk of ruining her new suit.

What else? Stockings to cover her legs or socks for warmer feet? Both. Along with her oxfords for when she took off her boots. A bar of soap and a tin of tooth powder, for sure, and maybe a deck of cards for something to do.

It was hard to know exactly what to take when she had no idea how long they'd be gone or where they would stay. Wherever that turned out to be, the place was sure to be full of strangers. What if she had a spell? What if there was nowhere to escape? What if everyone looked at her as if she were crazy?

The dress slipped from her hands, landing in a heap on the hardwood floor. She snatched it up impatiently. There had to be lavatories, right? She could go to the lavatory.

She gathered up everything she'd thought to pack and arranged it in the suitcase. When it appeared not much else would fit, she shut the lid to see how well it closed. The latches slipped easily into the locks. Room for a little more.

What would she feel better taking, rather than leave behind? Like her new silver bracelet, its square box already stowed in the gathered side pocket.

Her mind's eye roamed the house, conjuring up furniture, cabinets, closets. Nothing she might like to take was small enough to fit.

On top of the bedroom chest, the bronze frame holding her and Ben's wedding photograph reflected the candlelight. The photograph didn't have to be in a better light for her to picture Ben in the gray suit he still wore to Sunday Mass. Or see the posy of peonies clutched in her hands, brought up from his parents' farm. She'd designed and sewn her tea-length voile dress, and the savings had offset the cost of the intricate white lace she bought to drape over her hair.

She and Ben held the wedding breakfast at their new house, with Hank and an expecting Peachie doing the cooking as a wedding gift. Miranda's mother had hired a professional photographer, and he'd brought a backdrop to set up in the front room. The portrait was more than her mother could afford, but she wanted to commemorate the moment since she had no photograph at all of her own wedding.

The slim bronze frame would fit in the suitcase easily enough, but would it be safe? Would the glass get broken and scratch the photograph? She reached for the frame and noticed Ben's robe on the straight chair beside the chest.

He had tossed it there when he dressed for work the morning before – when she was upset with him for not staying home with her and Lucy. It hadn't taken long though, just a mention of no streetcars running, for her anger to melt into concern.

She left the photograph on the chest, picked up the robe, and shook it across the bed to fold the plaid flannel and tuck in the fraying sleeves. She wasn't sure why – maybe because she could bring the soft fabric up to her face and breathe in the solid assurance that was Ben – but she knew the robe would give her the solace she'd need that a photograph couldn't.

"I hope I haven't forgotten anything," she told Mr. Johnson a few moments later. She held her shivering arms up to the potbelly stove. "Clothes and toiletries and... oh, one more thing."

"Go ahead," he said. "I'll wait."

Not wanting to delay him any longer, she pulled herself from the warmth of the stove and took the flashlight to the sewing room. She had closed that door, and the one to the extra bedroom, to keep the warmth concentrated in the bathroom and her bedroom. If no boats came by before bedtime, she'd put Lucy in with her.

The air in the sewing room was as cold as the icebox in the pantry. The last quart of milk would easily stay fresh. Not that it mattered, since it would get wasted unless they stayed home long enough to drink it.

The beam of the flashlight flitted across the canned goods on the cutting table until it lit upon her tea tin. She laid the flashlight on its side and, opening the tin, pulled out the grocery money. She would keep it in her change purse. Lucy and the suitcase would be enough to manage without a pocketbook too.

She took a second to raise the shade at the side window and look out over the neighborhood for sign of a boat. The floodwater stretched across the yards to Peachie's house. Besieged by rain, the house no longer pulsed with life and light but sat dark and still and lonely.

An aching sadness pressed on Miranda, as if a thousand coats had been laid across her shoulders, only with no warmth. How would Peachie and Hank ever find it in themselves to return home without Henry?

~~~

She was sitting at her dressing table, writing a note to Ben by the beam of the flashlight, and Mr. Johnson was buttoning his jacket in the hallway, when the high-pitched drone of a motorboat carried across the floodwater. She looked up, and then across the room at Mr. Johnson.

"Want me to take the flashlight and flag it down?" he asked.

Her fingers tightened on the pencil. This is what Peachie would want, right? "Yes. I'll be down as quick as I can."

She carried the candle from the window and a handkerchief from Ben's chest drawer into the sewing room, where she filled the handkerchief with saltines and a wedge of cheese. She stuffed the food, which she hoped would get her and Lucy through to their next meal, into a corner of the suitcase and set the cat book on top.

She dressed them both for the outdoors, mindful of the weather and a boat trip in the open air. Lucy balked at having the tweed hat tied under her chin. Miranda tied on a warm headscarf and took a long, last look around the familiar bedroom. She blew out the candle.

The suitcase was heavier than she'd expected. With Lucy's mittened hand in her gloved one, she crossed the hall to the bathroom and turned down the wick of the coal oil lamp. The flame dwindled and died.

They took the dark stairway slowly. Baritone voices outside rose above an idling motor. Halfway through the front room, she stopped.

An invisible but palpable wall loomed between her and the door, a warning that it wasn't safe on the other side. She shrank back, unable to move beyond the impenetrable wall. Was it a mistake to leave after all? What danger awaited them?

She looked down at Lucy's hand, clinging tightly to her own. It had been days since Lucy had seen her mother, and she had no idea what was going on. Yet she trusted Miranda. She was depending on her. Miranda pushed through the wall and opened the front door.

A small skiff had landed on the porch steps, docked between the brick ledges on each side. Mr. Johnson shined the flashlight at a man in a black rain slicker whose hand gripped one of the ledges to anchor the boat. The flashlight moved up to the man's face, where the bill of his hat kept the rain off his glasses like an awning. Mr. Slatterman smiled at her.

"Fancy meeting you here," he quipped.

Disconcerted by a familiar face when she'd been expecting a stranger, she smiled wanly.

He tried again. "I understand Ben's not with you."

She cleared her throat and found her voice, raising it to be heard over the motor. "He never showed up from work this morning. I'm afraid something's happened to him."

"Ben's a capable young man," he reassured her. "He'll make it through."

It was kind of him to say so, but she wasn't convinced. Ben was capable, for sure, which was exactly why he should have made it home.

The skiff, a shallow boat with a pointed bow and square stern, rocked in the water that washed over the top porch step. The rescuer in the stern, a young man in only a jacket and toboggan cap to protect him from the rain, held the tiller that steered the boat. With the streetlights out, the night beyond him seemed endless.

"Where are we going?" she asked.

"A high spot at 18th and Broadway," said Mr. Slatterman. He reached for her suitcase and found a place for it between the seats. "From there, a truck will take you to the Armory."

The Armory. A chill shook her shoulders. Before she could say anything, Mr. Johnson picked up her umbrella from the porch floor and held it out to her along with the flashlight.

"I'll stay till the stove's burned down. Take good care of yourself and the little girl."

"Keep the flashlight. The house is dark, and I'm not sure how I'd manage it with everything else anyway." She pulled the change purse from her coat pocket and gave him the house key. "Would you lock up? I'll get the key from you when we come back home." Though it was hard to imagine when she'd see her house or neighbor again.

"Of course. I'll see all's well before I leave," he said.

Scooping up Lucy, he handed her to Mr. Slatterman, who set her gently on a flat board seat facing the stern. Miranda held onto the ledge and climbed into the rolling boat. She sat beside Lucy and opened the umbrella over their heads.

Mr. Johnson disappeared into the house. The other men pushed the skiff from the porch and powered up the engine. The boat backed into the yard, straightened, and headed into the street.

The block of Osage she knew as home disappeared into the darkness. Slatterman's grocery store, Peachie's house, St. Benedict's. The church was underwater, and the grocery store, not on a knoll like the houses, was inundated too.

Behind her, facing forward in the bow, Mr. Slatterman must have had similar thoughts. "It'll be a mess to come home to," he called, the wind carrying his voice to her.

She hoped he could see her nodding in sympathy.

The skiff sped down the next block of Osage, gliding between the utility poles that stuck out of the water. Mr. Slatterman had been right to face them backwards. Even with the umbrella situated more behind them than above, the cold wind seeped through her coat and whipped the scarf on her head. She pulled Lucy closer and, with a hand on the tweed hat and curls, nudged Lucy's head into the protection of her lap. Was this really the best way to keep her safe?

The smell of oil was strong in the night air, spilled from an unknown source to sprawl across the water. Chunks of ice swept past, along with trash cans that had drifted out of alleys, spewing bottles, boxes, and cans. She shuddered violently as a dead cat floated by. What had become of Pepper? Father Donovan hadn't been able to go looking for him.

"Help! Over here! We need a boat!"

Her eyes had grown accustomed to the darkness, and she turned to look. A man waved a towel from a second story window. The boat slowed.

"How many?" yelled Mr. Slatterman.

"Four! My wife! Two sons!"

"We'll have to come back! Hang on! We won't be long!"

Two more blocks down, the skiff turned onto 18th Street and joined the water traffic going north. The young man at the tiller made a wide pass around a makeshift raft and a long canoe. Both held the shadowy forms of more refugees, and neither had more to propel them than poles and oars.

The buildings on 18th Street – homes, churches, and the A&P – were all submerged to some extent. The glass dome of a gasoline pump poked above the water. A small yacht, ablaze with lights and churning great amounts of water, overtook them, sending a powerful wake their way.

"Hold tight!" hollered the young man, slowing the skiff.

The skiff rocked brutally. Miranda leaned over Lucy, her fingers digging into the wood seat. The young man maneuvered the wake at an angle, and the rocking gradually slowed.

Broadway, when they reached it, was like a river, and the boat fought its way across the current to reach the high spot on the other side. Lanterns brightened the corner. A policeman stood guard over the refugees on the sidewalk, his head frequently turning north to look up the unflooded stretch of 18th Street.

The bottom of the skiff scraped pavement. Miranda jerked, and Lucy popped up. Mr. Slatterman and the young man clambered out, wading in their rubber boots to push the boat closer.

Mr. Slatterman set Lucy on the sidewalk then held Miranda's arm to help her out. "I don't guess you've heard anything more about Henry," he said quietly.

"I have, and it's not good," she whispered. She couldn't force herself to repeat Mr. Johnson's words about Last Rites.

A pained look dimmed the optimism in Mr. Slatterman's eyes. "Stay at the Armory tonight," he said, setting the suitcase at her feet, "and see if you can get to Dolores's house tomorrow. They'll make room for you there, and you'll be better off."

She was afraid to ask what he meant by better off and asked for the house number instead.

He encouraged her, as Mr. Johnson had, to take care, then shoved off with the other rescuer and sped back toward Osage to pick up the stranded family. *Cindy Lou* was painted in large letters on the stern of the skiff. Somewhere, the young man at the tiller had a sweetheart.

She turned away from the flooding and lowered the umbrella until it rested against her headscarf. Hidden under its protection, she hugged Lucy close and sneaked a look at the other refugees clustered tensely on the corner in small groups. Not one person in front of the closed and darkened pharmacy looked familiar.

She was truly on her own.

~~~

A set of headlights bore through the darkness, and a large, rumbling vehicle drove up 18th Street. The truck turned left, stopped, and backed up to the corner.

The policeman on duty strode among the clusters of refugees, waving his arms and directing people to get on. The slat-sided truck reminded Miranda of one she'd seen hauling pigs to the Bourbon Stock Yard. Averse to being herded anywhere, she let the others go ahead of her.

A man with his belongings tied in a sheet slung them to the bed of the truck and jumped on. Leaning out, he helped a couple lift their three grade-school-age daughters onto the truck, each girl holding tight to the folded blanket in her arms. Their mother handed them an umbrella before she pulled herself up, and the girls took it to a corner and crowded beneath it.

The rest of the refugees climbed on or were helped on, the women attempting to maintain their modesty, and the older folks groaning from the exertion. Miranda hung back and watched. Maybe the truck didn't really carry livestock, or the gate would have been long enough to reach the ground and become a ramp. The policeman looked over and motioned her forward.

"Let's go," he said, an impatient edge to his voice. "There's still room."

She moved toward him, her legs barely supporting her. He hoisted Lucy onto the truck, but Miranda refused his help and got up on her own. She laid the suitcase flat for Lucy to sit on then huddled next to her on the wet planking.

The driver lifted the gate and fastened it, penning them in the truck bed until he would open it again. Miranda trembled uncontrollably, the umbrella shaking over her and Lucy's heads. She glanced around to see if anyone noticed, but the refugees' faces, even those of the children, were drawn inward.

The truck pulled away, picking up speed as it drove north on 18th Street. Families pulled in closer to stave off the wind and adjusted their umbrellas to keep them from blowing away. A few blocks up, the truck rounded the corner at Walnut and headed east toward downtown. Everyone shifted, either putting a hand to the floor to brace themselves or grabbing the side slats to hang on. Miranda tightened her arm around Lucy's waist, but her worry was fixed more on where they were going.

Mr. Slatterman had said they'd be taken to the Armory. She knew the Armory housed the National Guard, but because of its size – an entire city square – most people thought of it as the place that hosted city events. The Armory held thousands and thousands of people.

She hadn't been inside since she was five and her parents had taken her to a memorial service for the victims of the Titanic. She'd been jostled and squashed by the huge crowd and separated from her parents for a short but terrifying time. She'd never gone back, refusing even when Peachie begged her to attend a performance by Tommy Dorsey and his orchestra.

All weekend, people had been evacuating the West End in droves. No telling how many had sought refuge at the Armory. Would she be able to deal with a crowd that large? For even one night?

If only she could stop shaking. She wouldn't be any good to Lucy if she couldn't think straight. If she couldn't control herself. If she fell apart.

The truck approached the taller buildings of the business district. The streetlights were out there as well, though warmly lit windows in a few of the buildings revealed that not everyone had lost their electricity. At Sixth Street, the truck slowed, and the driver pulled into an open spot across from the front entrance to the Armory. A uniformed soldier whose rank she couldn't guess crossed the street to talk to him.

"We're bursting at the seams," the soldier called over the rain. "Try the hotels."

The hotels. She sagged toward Lucy, rain spilling from the umbrella. They wouldn't have to stay at the Armory. A hotel sounded so much better too. They'd have a room of their own, with privacy.

But what would it cost? A sick feeling in her stomach told her she couldn't pay for a room, not even for one night, at a downtown hotel and still have money for food. In the dining room alone, her money wouldn't last beyond a few meals.

They turned and parked in front of the Seelbach. This time the truck driver cut off the engine and walked up to the canopied entrance. Plodding like a man of sixty rather than the forty he appeared to be, he disappeared inside the hotel.

While the refugees waited for him to return, Miranda peered up and down Fourth Street. With all of the electric store signs turned off, it was scarcely recognizable. She'd seen a lot of out-of-the-ordinary things since they'd left home, but nothing as eerie as the street that typically was the busiest in town.

On a normal day, pedestrians crowded the sidewalks to shop the array of stores, visit a doctor or dentist in one of the office buildings, or eat lunch at a soda fountain or cafeteria. At night, marquees glowed brightly above theatergoers waiting expectantly in line. Tonight, Fourth Street was dark and deserted.

The last time she was downtown was the Friday evening before Christmas. Hank had piled everyone in the Ford to ride up and down Fourth Street and ooh and ah over the department store windows. Window dressers had filled the spaces behind the plate glass with lace and lights, Santas and sleighs, magical characters and make-believe snow. She and Peachie had squealed as delightedly as Lucy and Henry.

The truck driver emerged from the Seelbach, his demeanor lighter and his steps spryer than when he'd gone in. So it would be the hotel, whether she had the money or not. Maybe they could stay on credit, considering the circumstances.

The driver spoke to the refugees through the slats. "Full up, but there's still room at the Madrid. In the ballroom. I'll have you there in a jiffy."

The first murmurs of hope sounded throughout the truck. Miranda might have laughed if the situation were different. Peachie and Hank had partied at the Madrid on New Year's Eve. She and Ben had stayed home because she hadn't felt up to being in a crowd. Now, only three weeks later, she was going to the Madrid whether she liked it or not.

~~~

The truck traveled through floodwater on Chestnut Street then drove out of it, to her relief, when they turned onto Third. The driver slowed the truck as he reached the Madrid, parking at an angle so the headlights lit up the front of the building. When he came around and dropped the back gate, she slid off and helped Lucy down, urging her to stay close.

The refugees trooped down the sidewalk together, past the gaping black hole of the parking garage and up to the main doors. Beneath the darkened marquee, everyone's umbrellas came down, and they went inside.

The lobby was lit, but a sign posted by the elevator read *Shut Down*. No one complained about climbing the marble stairs, least of all Miranda. She was thankful not to be confined in an elevator and glad of the dry, quiet interior after what seemed an eternity in the rain aboard a noisy boat and truck.

On the second floor, the bowling alley and billiard rooms lay shadowy and hushed. The refugees climbed to the third, topmost floor and the ballroom where Hank and Peachie had danced.

In the third-floor foyer, doors led to the men's and women's restrooms, and a long table with five women seated behind it partially blocked the entrance to the ballroom. One of the women explained to the group – her monotone suggesting she'd done it many times over the course of the day – that each of them was required to register so the city could keep track of their whereabouts. Another woman informed them that the Red Cross was bringing in two meals a day, and there wouldn't be another until morning. No one mentioned money.

Miranda got into one of the lines and peeked inside the large ballroom to get a feel for where they'd be staying. Filigreed chandeliers, Spanish in appearance and hanging from a beamed ceiling, cast a mellow glow over the ballroom. Arched windows graced the room, and along the top of the high walls sat the romantic balconies Peachie had told her about.

As beautiful as it was, she worried whether she and Lucy would be safe. The downtown area, located along the river, seemed an unlikely place to be high and dry. The street out front wasn't flooded though, and she and Lucy were three stories up. They should be okay for the night, and they could leave for Dolores's house after they had breakfast in the morning.

At her turn, Miranda was asked to spell her and Lucy's names and give a home address.

"Find a cot and get yourselves situated for the night," the woman who took her information said. "You might have to share with the little girl." She didn't ask why Lucy's last name and address were different from Miranda's, evidently too weary to hear another refugee's troubling story.

Miranda picked up the suitcase and led Lucy into the ballroom. A few steps in, she paused to look around for a spot where they might be comfortable.

Tables covered the parquet dance floor in front of the bandstand, their bare tops unadorned by the snowy white tablecloths Peachie had described. Hundreds of cots surrounded the dance floor, set up all the way to the walls. The cots nearest the foyer and restrooms were taken.

Miranda guided Lucy to a side wall and found a single cot not far from the door. A wool blanket was folded on top, with no one's belongings nearby. She set the suitcase atop the brown canvas and her umbrella beneath, pleased to be at the edge of the crowd and in front of a window where she could see out.

On each side of the large, arched window, lush tapestries hung from rods attached to a painted-gold wall. The ballroom was as glamorous as Peachie had told her, though surely it was more accustomed to men in tuxedos and women with corsages pinned to their evening gowns than the wet and bedraggled souls taking refuge within its ornate walls at the moment.

She looked at the crowd more closely. No one had taken off their coats, and the men, abandoning good manners, had kept on their hats. There was no heat. The building had felt warm because they'd come in from the outdoors.

Lucy pulled at the ties on her tweed hat. Miranda untied them but insisted Lucy leave the hat on. She dried her with a bath towel, took off her wet shoes, and changed her damp socks.

Lucy studied the open suitcase. "Have my buttons?"

"I didn't bring them. Would you like to look at your cat book?"

Lucy shook her head. "I want buttons."

"There wasn't room for the button tin. I'm sorry."

A frown settled on the small, heart-shaped face. "I want buttons."

"I don't have them. They're at the house." Miranda said the words firmly, hoping to end the matter.

Instead, to her astonishment, Lucy crumpled to the floor and curled into a ball. "Mommy," she cried, her voice growing high and frantic. "I want my mommy."

Miranda looked helplessly at the sobbing heap. She felt the pressure of staring eyes. "Mommy's with Henry, remember?" She rummaged through the suitcase for Ben's handkerchief. "Would you like a cracker? Or some cheese?"

"No!"

Miranda pushed the suitcase to one side and sat down. She lifted Lucy onto her lap and, taking the hat from her red curls, pulled her close. The sobs quieted to a sniffle against Miranda's coat. She dropped her head and sang softly into Lucy's ear.

Lucy fell off to sleep. But only because she was exhausted, not because Miranda's singing came anywhere close to being as soothing as Peachie's. Or as accomplished.

Their freshman year in high school, Peachie had been chosen for a solo in the Christmas choral program, and then every year after until they graduated. At twenty, she won a talent contest at the local radio station. She could have made a career of singing if she wanted, but Hank was working at Ford by then and had enough money to buy her an engagement ring.

Hank wasn't the only one who fell in love with Peachie. She had sailed down the halls of Louisville Girls High with a smile and greeting for everyone she met, while Miranda, overwhelmed by the amount of girls and large classes in the overcrowded school building, stayed at the edge of the goings-on. She still wondered how, out of all the girls, she ended up Peachie's best friend.

Maybe because they both lost their dads the end of their freshman year. Peachie's dad hadn't died though. He walked out after a big fight with her mother and never came back.

The ballroom had grown quiet. One by one, the chandeliers were turned off until only one light, directed at the stage, dimly lit the room.

She pulled Lucy's nightgown out of the suitcase and smoothed the yellow flannel over the canvas cot. After easing Lucy onto the cot, her small face against the soft fabric, Miranda covered her with Ben's robe and added the scratchy wool blanket for warmth.

She didn't feel comfortable changing into a nightgown and robe, as one woman had. Besides, she wanted to be dressed and ready in case anything happened.

But what about brushing her teeth? Water wouldn't be rationed until morning, and the water from the restroom sinks would need to be boiled before anyone could use it.

She'd figure out something tomorrow. Or wait till she got to Dolores's. She closed the suitcase, sliding it under the cot along with her boots, and then laid beside Lucy. The stiff cot made it hard to get comfortable, much less relax and go to sleep.

The wooden frames creaked every time someone turned over in their cot. A man nearby breathed heavily in his sleep, producing an occasional deep snore, and two young women sat up still, whispering back and forth. Peachie would have gone over and joined them. All Miranda could think about was how peculiar it felt to be in a roomful of people making bedtime noises.

She slipped a hand into her coat pocket to feel for her change purse. Without warning, the ballroom went black. A woman's scream rang throughout the lofty ceiling. Miranda twisted her head toward the window. She could hear the rain, but there wasn't a light to be seen.

11

Monday, January 25, 1937

A firm hand nudged Miranda's shoulder, pulling her awake.

"Is something wrong?" she asked. An imagined catastrophe, always on the fringes of her mind, set her heart pumping.

"Please sit up," a female voice said crisply, "and take off your coat for a typhoid inoculation."

Miranda peered past the light that blinded her narrowed eyes. A nurse in a winged cap, holding a lantern, loomed over her. The sharp smell of alcohol cut through the stale air. Beyond the nurse, a doctor prepared to inoculate the man who'd been snoring. A second nurse, standing next to the doctor, held a tray with the bottles, bowls, and instruments he needed.

Miranda sat up and slipped out of her coat, trying not to wake Lucy. "Will she get an inoculation too?"

"How old?" the nurse asked.

"Three."

"Then, yes."

Good, they'd both be protected. Maybe the doctor could give Lucy her shot while she slept. Even if the sting woke her, the needle wouldn't have frightened her beforehand.

Miranda pushed on her sweater sleeve until it was bunched at the top of her arm. Shots weren't her favorite thing, and watching the dark-haired, mustachioed doctor hold the needle up to the lantern to check the amount of serum in the syringe didn't help. She scrunched her eyes as he took hold of her arm.

It wasn't as painful as she'd feared. Lowering her sleeve, she looked at the doctor, and then Lucy. "Could you give hers while she's sleeping?"

"How old is she?"

"Three," said the nurse, before Miranda had a chance.

He eased the covers off Lucy. "She's a little thing for three."

"She just had her birthday."

His long fingers rested on Lucy. "I'm not certain she weighs enough," he said, and covered her back up. "Rather safe than sorry." He moved on to the next cot.

Miranda opened her mouth to object. She wanted to call out and make him come back. But the three professionals, already giving up a night's sleep, were in a hurry to finish their job.

Wasn't this why she'd brought Lucy to a refugee center? Had it all been for nothing? If Lucy couldn't have the vaccine, was she in more danger than if they'd stayed at the house?

Sick with a miserable longing to be back home, Miranda edged under the covers and, with a shiver, pulled Ben's robe up to her cheek.

~~~

"More coffee?" The tall, imposing matron had helped herself to the percolator on the camp stove the Red Cross brought in. Her brown velvet hat, perched on silver waves, and the luxuriousness of her full-length mink coat suggested she had a maid to serve her coffee at home.

The man she'd asked shook his cap-covered head and swallowed his last bite of bacon. He hadn't spoken to anyone the entire meal, nor had his eyes left his plate.

The lady proceeded around the table. She skipped the young mother across from Miranda who not only wasn't drinking coffee but hadn't eaten. With a baby taking up her lap, she fed canned peaches to another child, not much bigger than a baby himself. When the young woman had a moment to spare, she brushed away the tears trickling down her cheeks.

The elderly couple at the end of the table nodded and smiled at the lady, as grateful for the extra coffee as when they'd said a blessing over their breakfast before they ate. Though they had bowed their fragile heads and prayed quietly, they were seated next to Miranda, and she'd heard the husband add an extra prayer for the protection of all the refugees driven from their homes by the terrible flood.

Miranda couldn't see the velvet-and-mink lady's face when she walked behind her and Lucy's chairs, but she may have been as surprised to see a glass of milk in front of Miranda as the Red Cross worker had been when Miranda chose it. After the spell on the train at Christmas, she knew better than to drink coffee and make herself more nervous than she already was.

She'd had to eat breakfast with her left hand, not thinking when she took the typhoid shot in her right arm that it would swell and then hurt when she moved it. The biscuits were good, if cold, and went down easy with the milk. Her stomach had contracted at the sight of the greasy bacon, and she'd skipped it.

On the other side of Lucy, the lady poured her husband a cup of the steaming coffee. A distinguished man who no doubt devoured the morning paper along with his breakfast, he appeared relieved to have something to occupy himself with now that he'd finished eating.

The hefty, cheerful man at that end of the table said "No, thanks" to more coffee, and the lady poured herself a cup before returning the percolator to the camp stove. The oddly happy man, who'd dominated the conversation with his stories throughout the meal, returned to the one he'd been telling.

"The water was so high that part of Broadway," he said, his voice blaring, "we had to duck under the traffic lights. Then, when I turned around to look back, I nearly capsized the boat." His laughter boomed across the table.

Even though Miranda found him painfully loud, she leaned toward him to distance herself from the conversation going on at the table behind her – a woman dramatically repeating a rumor that mass graves were being dug in Cave Hill Cemetery.

"That's not what I understood," a man's voice said. "I heard they're cremating all the dead bodies at Eastern Cemetery."

Miranda felt her face go white. *Please. Not Henry. Not Ben.* She would have returned to her cot if Lucy hadn't still been eating. Kneeling on a folding chair, Lucy looked up in surprise when Miranda leaned over and squeezed her close with her good arm.

Maybe they should stay at the Madrid one more night. Between her sore arm and upset stomach, she doubted whether she could make the long walk to Dolores's. She might wish later that they hadn't stayed – when the ballroom grew dark again and her thoughts along with it – but the Red Cross workers had told them the electric was out all across Louisville, so it would be off at Dolores's too.

It was hard to imagine everyone in the city making do without lights and electricity. Homes and stores, churches and hospitals. Her throat closed on a sip of milk.

Did an oxygen tent run on electricity?

~~~

She helped Lucy build houses with the playing cards for as long as she could sit up. Her nausea finally overwhelmed her, and she gave Lucy what was left of the cheese and saltines and lay down to watch her play and eat. More than a few of the refugees languished on their cots, their pallid faces evidence of the same queasiness she was feeling.

The rain had stopped before the Red Cross workers arrived with breakfast and, around noon, the first rays of sunshine streamed through the arched windows of the ballroom. The sunshine would have cheered her considerably if she hadn't felt so poorly.

She rolled onto her back, moaning as she roused the pain in her arm. Good thing she and Lucy had stayed put.

~ ~ ~

She woke with a start and, ignoring the pain, flipped on her side. The card houses, littered by cracker crumbs, had been abandoned. *No!* The word came out like a whimper. How could she have let herself fall asleep?

She struggled to her feet. The room tilted, and a stab in her stomach nearly doubled her over. People on the cots nearby glanced up.

"Did you see where she went?" Miranda asked one of the women.

"Your little girl? She said 'potty' and headed toward the restroom."

"How long has it been?"

"Well... a while now."

All but running, Miranda dodged cots and skirted chairs on her way to the foyer. When she'd taken Lucy to the restroom that morning, the water was on, and the toilets could be flushed to get rid of the waste that had accumulated. She cringed. The toilets would no longer be sanitary.

Please, please, be in the restroom. She ran into the foyer, her skin all that held her pulsing body together. No one was at the registration desk. Bursting into the restroom, she pushed on the stall doors that hung open and knocked on the ones that were locked. No one had seen a red-headed child.

Her sore arm banged into the door frame on the way out. She stopped to rub it and stared down the marble stairway. Surely she hadn't gone down there.

"Lucy! Lucy!" Miranda raced down the steps, her voice, higher-pitched than normal, ringing in the stairwell.

She reached the glass doors at the front entrance and pushed hard to get one open. Lucy wouldn't have had the strength. Still, Miranda went out to the sidewalk and glanced hurriedly up and down the sunny street.

By the time she searched the lobby and the second floor and made it back up to the ballroom, she was gasping for air and had to stop running. *Please, God. I'd rather die than tell Peachie something has happened to Lucy.*

Her eyes swept the room. It was no good – she'd never find her that way. She hurried to the far end of the ballroom, no longer caring if she could breathe or if anyone looked at her funny. Working her way back, she searched every group of refugees, scrutinized every cot and chair.

On the floor by one of the cots, a brass birdcage held three blue parakeets, balancing on swings. A thin woman in her fifties squatted beside the cage and murmured sweetly to the birds. A small hand reached out and touched one of the cherubs that decorated the cage.

"Stop that!" In an instant, the woman's tone changed from a fond whisper to a bark. "Little girls have no business bothering other people's things."

"Lucy!" Miranda rushed over and gathered her up, never so glad to feel the warmth of the tiny body against her own.

A powerful sensation welled up from within. Not panic, as she was used to, but anger. She stared into the woman's eyes, determined not to look away. "There was no need to talk to her like that."

The woman's eyes narrowed to slits. "Don't tell me what I should be doing. If you were any kind of mother, a child this age wouldn't be roaming around by herself."

Miranda lurched as if she'd been stabbed. She clutched Lucy tighter, her anger dissolving into a hollow kind of cold. She stumbled toward the foyer. She had to get away from the woman, away from everyone.

She took the marble stairs in a rush, not sure where she was headed. On the second floor, she ran into the bowling alley and moved quickly through the shadows. She couldn't hold on much longer.

Stopping at last in a far, dark corner, she let the tears come. She cried for herself, for Henry, and for Peachie, sobbing until there was nothing left to cry about. Lucy patted her back.

12

Tuesday, January 26, 1937

An explosion rattled the large windows along the walls, rousing anyone who wasn't already awake. Miranda pushed up and looked out, jumping as another explosion echoed across the city. Not downtown, but not far away.

A good number of refugees got up to crowd near Miranda's cot and stare out the arched windows that faced west. The distant sky lit up with an orange-red glow that outlined the buildings across the street. The glow heightened and swelled, as if the whole West End were on fire.

"The world is ending!" a woman shrieked.

"The world is not ending," her husband said gruffly, if only to silence her hysteria.

Miranda couldn't see flames, but the sky had brightened to a brilliant yellow beneath the reddish glow. Were she and Ben losing their home?

Every face, even the one of the cheerful man who sat at her table for meals, registered the fear that the fire might reach them at the Madrid. Hypnotized by the spectacle out the windows and bound to the building by the night, few moved until the sun came up and the Red Cross workers arrived with breakfast.

~~~

That afternoon, the velvet-and-mink lady brought Miranda a newspaper she and her husband had finished with, a bit of good fortune since everyone was anxious to get hold of one of the small number of copies. Ever since breakfast, when the refugees found out a varnish company at 14th and Maple had caught fire, Miranda wanted to know what was really happening instead of imagining the worst. Thick, black smoke still rose in the sky, but it turned out her house was no closer to the blaze than she was.

The flimsy newspaper, consisting of only four pages, had been published in Shelbyville, a small town to the east. The morning *Courier-Journal* and the evening *Louisville Times* were both named in the heading, and *Flood Edition No. 2* was printed across the top. The bold headline, "Martial Law is Declared in Louisville," startled her as much as the rest.

At Governor Chandler's request, federal troops were being sent in to help combat panic and pestilence in Kentucky. Scarlet fever and measles, the paper said, had already struck the refugees at Loew's Theater. Miranda glanced around at the other refugees, trying not to appear nosy and suspicious. She was thinking more and more that Lucy would have been better off at home.

Louisville police were ordered to shoot looters on sight, since everything in the stores, as well as gasoline at the oil stations, was needed to help the refugees. On a more positive note, radio stations across the country were raising funds for the flood victims. WWJ in Detroit had raised ten thousand dollars.

The Ohio River was at fifty-five feet, nearly double flood stage, and continued to rise. With two-thirds of the city inundated, everyone seemed to be holding a collective breath until the river crested.

A caption with the word "train" caught her eye. She pulled the paper closer and read faster. Maybe something in the article would give her a clue about Ben.

The previous day, refugees had been transported in boxcars from the Baxter Avenue Station to Crescent Hill. The East Louisville Yard, where Ben spent Saturday night, was adjacent to the Baxter Avenue station. Maybe the railroad had needed him so badly, he'd stayed and worked, hoping she would understand when he finally got home.

Large trucks had forded the floodwater surrounding the station and carried refugees to elevated walks which they crossed to enter the boxcars. "As the water continued to rise," she read, her eyes rushing down the page, "this was the last hope of escape from the marooned downtown section." The downtown area was marooned? As if they were on an island?

Maybe she and Lucy should leave for the East End while they could still get there. It would be a long walk to the Baxter Avenue Station, and then they'd have to walk from Crescent Hill to the Highlands, where Dolores lived. They could do that. It was the part about crossing Beargrass Creek that made her stomach start hurting again.

Trapped in a boxcar. A dark boxcar. Shoulder-to-shoulder with strangers. Across a raging creek.

Her shoulders twitched and shook her out of the imagined nightmare.

Another article said the river might not crest until it reached fifty-eight feet. If that turned out to be the case, only the Highlands, Crescent Hill, and a small area around City Hall would remain dry.

She and Lucy had to leave soon, or they'd be stuck at the Madrid until it was all over, and no telling how long that would be. But she couldn't think about the boxcars without her heart racing wildly.

~~~

The meal on the metal plate in front of her consisted of a thin slice of ham, a dollop of jelly, and a spoonful of beans. At least the meager portions would fill Lucy. And thankfully, the young mother across from them was finally eating. Her baby was fussy though, and the mother apologized, saying it was hard to keep him in clean diapers. After dinner, Miranda sought her out and gave her the extra bar of soap and second bath towel she and Lucy had no need of, encouraging her to cut or tear the towel into diapers.

The sun dropped into the smoke still billowing in the west. With the ballroom growing dark and only a few lanterns available, the refugees settled into their evening routines. She and Lucy played a game of *I'm Going on a Trip*.

The quiet was broken when a man with a medical bag strode in from the foyer, his flashlight cutting through the dimness. Two men in white uniforms followed – ambulance drivers, since one of the men carried an empty stretcher. Miranda sat up straighter as the three men were met by the woman who'd registered her and Lucy Sunday evening. She led the men to a nearby section of the room.

Whatever was going on had to be more serious than a reaction to a typhoid inoculation. Miranda's own nausea was gone when she woke that morning, and she felt lighter all over. Maybe crying things out had helped too.

The men were taken to a boy about Henry's age. The similarity ended there, the boy being blond and husky. The doctor set his black bag on the floor and opened it, pulling out a thermometer he shook down and put in the boy's mouth. He lifted the boy's shirt and used the flashlight to examine his chest.

Except for a few whispers and the scraping of chair and cot legs against the floor as the refugees shifted to see better, the ballroom had grown completely still. The doctor's words carried clearly to Miranda.

"Definitely measles. We need to get him to the contagion hospital."

"Contagion hospital?" asked the boy's mother.

"At a church in Crescent Hill," said the doctor. "All cases of contagious disease are being held there."

The boy's father put his arm across his wife's shoulders and whispered in her ear. She nodded, but whatever he said didn't take the worry from her face.

The doctor removed the thermometer and rolled it between his fingers to read how high the mercury had risen. He signaled to the ambulance drivers. They lifted the boy onto the stretcher, and his parents followed them out to the foyer.

As soon as the family was out of sight, voices rose throughout the room – worried voices of people concerned about the spread of measles. Miranda walked up to the window. The lights were still out across the city, but the street below, under a luminous full moon in a clear sky, was lit enough to watch the ambulance drive away.

Measles spread easily, she knew, and it could be dangerous too. The children who'd played with the boy might already be coming down with it. Lucy hadn't been one of them, but the Madrid was no longer safe.

13

Wednesday, January 27, 1937

At breakfast, Miranda asked the Red Cross worker who was leaving the latest flood edition of the newspaper on their table if she knew whether the trains from the Baxter Avenue station to Crescent Hill were still running.

"I'm not sure," said the girl, the same age as the Slattermans' Ruth Anne but with a more serious look in her eyes. "I do know there's a way to walk to the East End now. She leaned forward, her face alight with the opportunity to tell what she knew. "A pontoon bridge has been built across Beargrass Creek."

"A what?" asked the velvet-and-mink lady, her long arm reaching for the newspaper.

"A pontoon bridge. It's for foot traffic, and it's floating on empty whiskey barrels. My friend saw the men building it yesterday. It starts at the end of Jefferson Street and goes along Baxter Avenue until the street rises out of the floodwater."

"So all we have to do," Miranda asked, her eagerness making her more talkative than she'd been at any other meal, "is go down there and take the bridge across?" That would mean no boxcars, and she and Lucy wouldn't have as far to walk to Dolores's.

"That's what I understand," said the young woman. "Jefferson is one of the few streets that isn't flooded between here and the creek." Her gaze dropped to the newspapers in her arm and, with a guilty start, she took off to distribute them.

~ ~ ~

Miranda and Lucy weren't the only ones walking down the marble staircase after breakfast. Dozens of others had packed up their belongings after hearing about the pontoon bridge, including the velvet-and-mink lady and her husband, forced to leave their Packard downtown and walk with the rest of the refugees.

Miranda would have preferred to wait until the temperature warmed up, but any number of things might delay them, and she wanted to arrive at Dolores's well before dark. They might stop and eat at some point, maybe at one of the canteens she'd told Ben about, and she couldn't expect Lucy to walk all that way without resting now and then.

The large, cheerful man held the front door, and she stepped with Lucy out to the sidewalk. After three days in an unventilated building, with the smell of cigarette smoke, body odor, and unflushed toilets fouling the ballroom, the morning air felt exceptionally fresh. The cold made it even more so. She drew in a deep breath to fortify herself for what lay ahead.

The refugees headed north on Third Street, passing out of the shade cast by the Madrid Building and into the brilliant sunshine brightening Guthrie Street. Lucy's mittened hands flew to her eyes. Miranda squinted and looked up the street before they crossed. Patches of ice floated on a pool of sparkling floodwater less than a block away. They crossed to the next corner. Trinity Church towered over them and put them back in the shade.

"Are you warm enough?" she asked Lucy.

Lucy shivered and shook her head.

Miranda squatted and picked her up. It felt good to walk after being confined for days, but she wasn't sure how far she could carry Lucy in addition to the suitcase and umbrella. Walnut, Liberty, and then Jefferson, she counted in her head.

"Just a few blocks and we'll be walking into the sunshine. That will warm us up."

The refugees made no effort to stay together. By the time they reached the meat markets and egg houses on Jefferson Street, where policemen with weary faces guarded the stores, the faster walkers were a block ahead, and the older, slower ones lagged behind.

Miranda's arms ached, and she put Lucy down on the sidewalk. Up ahead, steam rose in wispy white puffs above a square of stacked bricks. A sturdy stick had been placed across the bricks, and a black pot hung from the stick by its handle. A small fire blazed beneath the pot. The rich aroma of coffee wafted up as they walked past. The familiar smell lifted her spirits, as did the bright sun on her face.

A number of empty automobiles sat parked along the curb of the cobblestone street, seemingly abandoned. The few that did speed past were impromptu emergency vehicles, sporting swathes of red cloth over their front headlights. Large trucks hauling soldiers and supplies rumbled more slowly over the streetcar tracks, the tracks useless without electricity.

The sidewalk was far more crowded than the street, and Miranda stayed to one side, near the curb. Across Jefferson Street, a line had formed outside the Liberty Restaurant. A temporary sign set up in front designated the restaurant a Hot Food Center, run by the Salvation Army. The line of people waiting for a meal wound around the corner.

She considered for a moment whether to cross over and eat while they had the chance. It hadn't been that long since breakfast though, and the lines might not be as bad once they reached the Highlands. Since Lucy seemed content to be swept along by the crowd, Miranda switched the suitcase to her other hand and kept going.

They had a lot of walking ahead of them, and she hadn't walked as far since high school. In the summer, when Peachie wasn't working or watching her younger brothers while her mother was at the race track, and when Miranda didn't have some chore or sewing to keep her at the apartment, the two would entertain themselves by taking day-long treks, sometimes miles out Cane Run Road. On Sundays, they walked to Shawnee Park to watch Hank play baseball.

That was before Hank's mother introduced Miranda to Ben. He moved to Louisville her senior year and took a room in the boarding house Mrs. Ryan opened when Hank's dad died. Not long after Miranda and Ben started dating, Hank bought an old jalopy and toted the four of them around town. She hoped she still had the legs to make the long walk ahead.

They neared the end of Jefferson Street. Beyond it, across Baxter Avenue, lay the L&N's East Louisville Yard. Despite her resolve to remain calm, Miranda's step quickened. Maybe, just maybe, Ben would be there.

~~~

A supply truck with a load of steel milk cans in its bed pulled away from the edge of the floodwater at Jefferson and Baxter and headed downtown, leaving wet tire tracks on the cobblestones. As soon as Jefferson Street was clear to cross, the refugees walked over to the north side where the pontoon bridge began.

Instead of following, Miranda took Lucy's hand and kept walking alongside the brick shotgun houses and postage-stamp front yards to their right. The sidewalk kept her and Lucy clear of the floodwater another half block, and she hoped to get a better view of the railroad yard.

But all she could see beyond the pontoon bridge, which passed between them and the East Louisville Yard, was more floodwater and the tops of stranded boxcars. The yardmaster, the one person who might know where Ben was, couldn't possibly be in his office.

She turned to lead Lucy back to where they could cross the street. The front door of one of the shotgun houses opened, and a man came out and stopped on the front steps. He raised his arms and positioned a striped cap on his thick, black hair. His denim jacket, hanging open over his overalls despite the cold temperatures, showed a red plaid tie knotted beneath a spotless white collar. A railroader. Maybe he knew Ben.

She would have preferred approaching a kindly conductor, or even a crusty engineer, but this dapper railroader might be her only chance to find out where Ben was. Clearing the hesitation from her throat, she approached him.

"Excuse me. Do you work for the L&N? My husband is a fireman for the railroad, and I've lost touch with him. I was hoping you might know him."

His dark eyes flashed appreciation as he looked into her own. "And who would this lucky man be?"

"Ben Kinley," she answered, struggling to hold his gaze.

"Ben! That devil! I see now why he's kept you hidden away." He grinned, showing crooked teeth that didn't diminish his handsomeness. "Maybe he's mentioned me. The boys call me Scrappy."

Scrappy. Oh, yes. The engineer who had a way with women. She glanced at the shotgun house, and then down at the sidewalk. "Y…yes, he tells me about the other men at work."

His sudden and close attention made her feel as trapped and afraid a spell would come on as if she'd been enclosed in an elevator. She put down the suitcase and picked up Lucy to break the tension.

"Have you seen him recently?"

"Sure. Last weekend. He told Ol' Jenkins on Sunday he was headed home to make sure you were okay. He said he'd come back if he could. No one's seen him since."

"Oh." The word dropped quietly between them. Her insides shrank. She hadn't truly expected to find Ben at the railroad yard, but she'd set her hopes on finding out he was helping with the rescue work *somewhere*.

"Thank you." She grabbed the suitcase handle and fled up the sidewalk with Lucy before Scrappy could say anything else she'd be required, out of politeness, to answer.

~~~

She couldn't allow herself to think where Ben might be. Or imagine what went wrong Sunday morning between the railroad yard and home. Later maybe, at Dolores's house when she had a few moments alone, but not now.

The refugees crowded at the foot of the pontoon bridge. From the other side of the street, she hadn't been able to see that the bridge was four blocks long. Or notice it was so narrow, people were crossing single file. But mostly she hadn't thought about how, once she got on, she couldn't get off.

What if she had a spell before they made it to the end? There'd be nowhere to go. Nowhere to get away.

She realized she'd stopped walking when people started going around her to get to the bridge. People who had no trouble getting on and traipsing doggedly across. Why did she have to be so different? So incapable? And what was she going to do?

She couldn't take Lucy back to the Madrid, not as long as there was a risk of measles. They *had* to cross the bridge. She glanced nervously at the people to each side of her and started walking again.

The bridge was tethered to the utility poles on one side of Baxter Avenue, leaving room on the remainder of the flooded street for boats to bring boxes of supplies and bags of mail to the downtown area. At the edge of the water on Jefferson Street, not far from where she and Lucy waited their turn to get on the bridge, four men in knee-high boots carried a casket into the water and set it in one of the emptied boats. They returned to their truck and unloaded a second casket.

She couldn't stop watching. Who lay inside the coffins? How had they died? The refugees pressed in, everyone pushing to get to the bridge. Her eyes darted from the steel caskets to the frigid floodwater and back to the long, crowded bridge.

I can't do this. I just can't.

She drew Lucy away, threading a hurried path through the crush and across the street. Her shoe caught the edge of a cobblestone, and she fell against a parked automobile. A pain shot through her chest. Tears rushed to her eyes.

Why had she ever thought she could take care of Lucy away from the safety of home? This was exactly why she'd told Ben she couldn't adopt. If she couldn't do a simple thing like walk Lucy across a bridge, how could she take care of a child all its growing-up years?

"I'm tired." Lucy looked up at her pitifully.

"I know, sweetie." Miranda blinked, but the warm tears spilled onto her cheeks anyway.

Lucy's eyes grew worried. She circled Miranda's legs with her mittened hands and rested her cheek on Miranda's coat. "I'm sorry."

Miranda wrapped an arm around the slight shoulders. Her chest ached again, but with tenderness this time. *I'll take good care of Lucy.* The assurance she gave Peachie came to mind, and the words summoned a surge of strength.

"You've no reason to be sorry. Let's go cross that bridge, and then we'll find someplace to rest."

Two soldiers had directed the refugees to form a line. She walked Lucy resolutely to the end of it, quietly observing those already waiting.

A boy about twelve, struggling to keep his tan-and-white mutt from running off, wrapped the faded belt he'd substituted for a leash twice around his hand. An older man, thin and unkempt, balanced a soiled mattress on his head, while a man she recognized from the Madrid kept a safe distance behind the mattress. Near the end of the line, a young couple craned their necks to check the progress, eager looks brightening their fresh faces.

"Not long now," Miranda heard the young woman say.

"Yessiree," said her husband. "A warm house, a clean bed, and one of your mother's hot meals. I can't wait." He smiled at his wife good-naturedly.

His words stayed with Miranda as she and Lucy got into line. That was the way *she* needed to look at things. She needed to think about all the good that would happen once they were on the other side.

Such as how, once they reached Dolores's house, they'd be with people who knew them and cared about them. They'd get to sleep in a quiet bedroom, not a crowded ballroom. On a comfortable mattress and not a stiff cot. There would be Mrs. Slatterman to deal with, of course, but no doubt she'd welcome them with open arms.

It shouldn't take much more than fifteen minutes to cross the bridge, even with everyone carrying parcels and trying to keep their footing. After that, they'd be in the Highlands and on their way. And she'd finally get to see Dolores's house.

Mrs. Slatterman had told her bits and pieces about the house ever since Dolores married and moved to the East End. The wide front porch that swept around one side. The tower room on the second floor. Five bedrooms and a huge kitchen. It would be a wonderful place to stay until the flood was over.

Good friends. A warm house. A quiet bedroom. Good friends. A warm house. A quiet bedroom. Repeating the words in her head shaved the edge off her fear.

She was close enough now to get a better look at the pontoon bridge. The Red Cross worker had been right about the empty whiskey barrels. The barrels floated inside wooden frames down the length of the bridge. A boardwalk ran across the top of the frames, and two-by-fours stuck up on each side with a rope handrail threaded through. She'd have preferred something more substantial than a rope.

By the time their turn came to get on the bridge, her heart couldn't have been beating any harder. She and Lucy followed the other refugees up the ramp and stepped onto the narrow boardwalk. The wooden structure felt solid at first but, as they moved off land, the bridge rolled with the current.

Working quickly, so as not to hold up the line, she took off Lucy's mittens and her own gloves for a better grip on Lucy's hand. With the suitcase and umbrella in her other hand, she balanced the best she could.

The dazzling sunshine, warm against her headscarf, sparked flashes of gold on the rippling brown water. Her legs were shaky, but she kept moving – and prayed everyone else would too. She'd be okay as long as the line didn't stop.

Once the bridge left Jefferson Street and crossed over to follow Baxter, the railroad yard was on their left. Two men in a fishing boat rowed along a side track lined with boxcars. Neither was Ben. She could recognize him from farther away than that.

The pontoon bridge stayed beside the rail yard until it reached the normal boundaries of Beargrass Creek. There, the current pushed harder against the bridge. She grabbed onto the rope handrail with the fingers she could spare from the suitcase and umbrella.

The wind strengthened too, catching the mattress on the old man's head and tilting it to one side. He yanked it in the other direction then teetered wildly back and forth. The bridge pitched with him. The tan-and-white dog yelped, straining against its leash, and everyone grabbed for the handrails.

The rope jerked from Miranda's hand. She lost hold of the suitcase and umbrella. Both fell from the lurching bridge, glanced off the wooden frame, and landed in the floodwater. The umbrella sank, tip first, and the leather suitcase, hopelessly out of reach, turned on its side and floated away.

No!

She braced herself on one of the two-by-fours. None of the supply boats were close enough to wave down. The suitcase sailed across the floodwater and slammed into a light pole. It hung only a second before drifting down the street.

She'd never get it back. There wasn't a tag on the handle where she could have put their name and address, and the initials on her silver bracelet weren't enough to help a stranger find her. Ben's robe. Lucy's cat book. Their clothing and toiletries. How would she and Lucy make do without it all?

The refugees had righted themselves, and the line started moving again. Miranda walked numbly to the end of the boardwalk and down the ramp. She let loose of Lucy's hand. If she'd held on too tight when the bridge started pitching, Lucy hadn't complained.

"Give 'em room!" shouted a soldier with a rifle slung over his shoulder. He directed the order at a crowd of people who'd bunched at the end of the ramp to anxiously search the faces of the itinerant refugees for loved ones.

"Over here! Here I am, dears!"

At the far edge of the crowd, a woman in a dark coat with a large fur collar waved a handkerchief above her head. A few steps ahead of Miranda, the good-natured young man and his wife shouldered through the crowd and into her embrace.

The bricks of Baxter Avenue felt solid and reassuring beneath Miranda's feet. It pleased her that things had turned out for the young couple as they'd hoped. And now that she and Lucy had made it safely across the bridge, the suitcase didn't seem quite as important.

~~~

Louisville Railway buses, each an agreeable green and cream, lined Baxter Avenue's hill. She'd had no idea so many city buses existed. Bus lines had increased in recent years, but streetcars were the more common sight.

A smattering of Fayette County school buses also awaited the refugees. Getting on one would mean a seventy mile trip to Lexington. Thank goodness she and Lucy had someplace else to go.

"Let's take a bus to Dolores's," she said to Lucy. "We can rest a bit and save ourselves the walk too."

Overhead, a sputtering noise grew closer and louder until everyone on the street had raised their faces to the clear, blue sky to see what was causing the roar. Lucy stretched out her arm and pointed.

"Airplane!"

Miranda shielded her eyes from the sun. A bi-plane was flying much too close to the electrical and telephone lines for her comfort. A pilot maneuvered the plane from the cockpit in back, while another man hung out the front seat with a megaphone. His words, nearly overpowered by the sound of the engine, became clear at last.

"The Ohio River has crested! Fifty-seven-point-one-five feet at two o'clock this morning. The Ohio River has crested!"

The bi-plane soared off, its sputter dying slowly away. A teenager's cheer broke the awestruck silence, and an older gentleman whisked off his cap and threw it straight up in the air.

~~~

She gave up looking for a Bardstown Road bus after she'd checked the destination signs on the front of three city buses and they all said *SPECIAL*. At the next bus, she leaned in the open door and asked the driver where he was headed.

"A refugee center. At a church on Bardstown Road."

"Oh, good. That's where we need." She inquired if the street Dolores lived on was anywhere near the church.

"Same neighborhood," he assured her. His amiable brown eyes, blinking behind a pair of familiar glasses, made her think of Mr. Slatterman.

She helped Lucy up the bus steps, and then reached into her coat pocket, pulling out mittens and gloves before she got to her change purse.

"No fares for the refugees," the driver said with a smile. "Find yourself a seat."

A spot on the aisle and near the door was unoccupied. She took it at once and settled Lucy in her lap. The plump, friendly woman she sat down beside chatted with the woman behind them.

Refugees young and old sank gratefully into the remainder of the seats. The driver steered from the curb, and the bus lumbered up Baxter Avenue. They passed storefronts and apartment buildings until Eastern Cemetery appeared on the left. The crematorium, an imposing structure, sat near the front gate.

Though sunshine fell generously on the cemetery, thoughts of the breakfast conversation at the Madrid about the crematorium stole Miranda's short-lived sense of well-being. She and Lucy might be safely away from the flooding, but she still had no idea where Ben was or, even more worrisome, how Henry was doing.

At the edge of Eastern Cemetery, Cave Hill came into view, the much larger cemetery where the woman had said mass graves were dug. The bus grew warm and stuffy. Miranda untied her headscarf and slipped it off her head. If she hadn't promised Lucy a rest, she would have pulled the cord to get off and walked the rest of the way.

"Oh, good! I can finally set my watch!" The plump woman, brushing against Miranda, turned back around to peer out the window.

A broad driveway curved up to Cave Hill's park-like entrance, and a clock tower flanked the stone building on the left. Ten minutes to ten. Surely it was later in the morning than that. Hadn't they left the Madrid hours and hours ago?

All at once, Miranda grew lightheaded and trembly. Either she was hungry, or she was worrying more than was good for her about Henry and Ben. She took a deep breath and let it out slowly.

They veered onto Bardstown Road. Traffic was heavy, and it didn't help that a large truck had been abandoned in the middle of the street. The bus slowed and maneuvered around it.

At the corner, a crowd had collected on the sidewalk. Newspaper pages were pasted to the plate glass window of the Piggly Wiggly, and a man near the window called out the headlines to those in the back.

Up a few more blocks, the traffic light was out at Eastern Parkway, reminding her that the East End had no electric service either. A policeman, wearing a uniform other than that of the Louisville police, directed traffic. Pointing and waving, he confidently handled the buses, emergency vehicles, and farm trucks bringing milk to town.

"I'll be!" the plump woman said to her. "He looks like an English bobby with that chin strap on his hat!"

The bus crossed Eastern Parkway and entered the Bonnycastle neighborhood. Bonnycastle always made her think of Parkland – a shopping district surrounded by stylish homes. Except Parkland was flooded up to its porches.

Bardstown Road seemed unusually busy. The bus could have been on Fourth Street, with all the people parading up and down the sidewalks. Not shopping, since the stores weren't open, but greeting one another and enjoying the sunshine and the freedom of walking outside now that it had stopped raining.

Her seat mate called out again, this time to no one in particular. "Oh! There's my hairdresser! I'm so glad to know she's okay!"

Miranda hadn't been paying close attention to the faces on the sidewalks, but she scanned them earnestly now, watching for a young man with sandy hair who'd be taller than most.

The traffic moved slowly, and she had time to read a notice posted on a drug store window. *Boil all water, or add one drop iodine to a quart of water and shake. Let stand five minutes before drinking.* She grimaced. Iodine didn't sound very appetizing.

A familiar face passed in front of the drug store, and Miranda nearly lifted Lucy out of the seat. "Look!" She pointed out the window. "It's Ruth Anne!" But Ruth Anne was lost in the crowd before Lucy could spot her.

A booth had been set up on the sidewalk in front of a large Baptist church. The wooden structure was covered with a canvas tarp. Lanterns hung from the frame, and Army blankets were folded on tables beneath the tarp. A teenager walked up to the booth, and a soldier gave him a blanket.

She'd been watching the street signs as well as the people and gasped with satisfaction when the bus passed Dolores's street. Not knowing how much farther to the refugee center, she started counting the blocks. A short time later, the driver pulled the bus to the curb. He eased himself up from his seat and turned to face the refugees.

"You can get a hot meal inside. The homes in the neighborhood are full, so transportation is being provided to towns outside the city where you can stay until it's safe to return home."

Miranda's arms tightened around Lucy. The homes in the neighborhood were full. She'd never even considered that.

~~~

She didn't get to Bardstown Road that often and was surprised every time she saw St. Francis of Assisi. The Catholic church, set back on a gracious lawn, had a facade reminiscent of the Alamo. An arched portico, round-top windows, and red tile roof, all resplendent in the abundant sunshine, added to the feeling that they'd arrived at a southwestern mission. But a cold breeze, ruffling her hair and stealing down her neck, quickly brought her back to Kentucky.

While the other refugees from the bus tramped up the broad sets of steps leading to the church, she hesitated on the sidewalk, wondering what to do next. She'd looked so forward to arriving at Dolores's, and now she was afraid they'd find there was no room for them. If she and Lucy had no place to stay, they'd be sent out of town to lodge with strangers.

Lucy's face was paler than usual. A hot meal would give them both some needed strength. They'd eat first then go to Dolores's and, if they were lucky, there'd still be an extra bed.

Trailing the others, they climbed the broad steps, crossed the portico, and entered the vestibule. A Sister greeted them with a hello and a nod of her veiled head. Her long, black habit nearly brushed the terrazzo floor.

"This way, please." Her milk-white hand, extending from the end of a wide sleeve, pointed them to a stairwell. The steps led down to a cafeteria which, though spacious enough, was crowded. The din nearly turned Miranda back.

A registration table, much like the one at the Madrid, was set up perpendicular to the doorway, with volunteers seated behind it signing people in. The young woman who took Miranda's and Lucy's information wrote with sure, quick strokes.

"Have you had any typhoid inoculations?"

"Yes. Sunday night – or early Monday morning. During the night, anyhow."

"Two days ago. Then you'll need a second one in eight days. The Health Department is spacing the shots farther apart because of the reactions people are having. And the child?"

"She's old enough, but the doctor was concerned she didn't weigh enough. She wasn't given one."

The young woman, though she'd undoubtedly had her own inoculation, sat ever so slightly back. "Do you have somewhere to stay?" she asked crisply.

"I'm not sure. We might. Is it okay if we have something to eat first?"

"Of course. There's a convoy of automobiles leaving for Campbellsville at two o'clock. You'll need to figure out your sleeping arrangements before then. We've run out of room for cots in the schoolrooms."

Miranda led Lucy toward the eating tables in the middle of the cafeteria. On the far wall, the typhoid shots were being given at a doctor's station. Along another wall, volunteers were opening boxes of food and distributing it. Long tables lined a window wall, where more volunteers rummaged through piles of clothes and shoes to help refugees find what they needed.

Clothing! She could get Lucy a nightgown and underwear–

"Miranda!"

A vaguely familiar voice called from somewhere in the cafeteria.

"Miranda!"

This time, the voice carried clearly across the commotion. A petite woman with salt-and-pepper hair thrust a pair of shoes at a refugee and ran up the aisle between two rows of eating tables. When Mrs. Broome reached them, she caught Miranda firmly by the arms.

"I can't believe you're here!"

The last time Miranda had seen Father Donovan's housekeeper, she was driving off with the Sisters from St. Benedict's. What was she doing at St. Francis of Assisi, and why would someone usually so reserved act like this?

"Everyone is worried sick about you and Lucy! We were afraid something horrible had happened to you."

Miranda shook her head. Shouldn't everyone be more worried about Henry? Unless... The room swirled, and the din grew muffled. She stumbled to an empty chair at one of the tables.

"When's the last time you've eaten?" Mrs. Broome hovered over her.

"This morning." Miranda gathered Lucy in her lap to reassure her. "But we walked a long way, and we're both tired and hungry."

"Sit still. I'll bring you something." She set off briskly for the kitchen. Rather than wait in the meal line, Mrs. Broome disappeared in the back and came out a short time later with two plates of steaming stew.

"Coffee?"

"Milk for both of us, please."

As soon as Mrs. Broome brought the milk, Miranda lifted her glass and drank it all down. Then she started on the beef stew, pushing aside the nagging thoughts about what horrible thing could possibly have happened to them. It was more reassuring to watch Lucy eat and be glad of the color returning to her cheeks.

"I saw you leave with the Sisters Saturday morning," she finally said.

Mrs. Broome had quit fussing over them and sat across the table with a cup of coffee.

"Ben was supposed to be home from work that evening, but he stayed overnight at the railroad yard, and then he didn't show up Sunday morning like he was supposed to. When the rain started again, the water backed up in the storm drains, and the whole neighborhood flooded. Mr. Johnson came over–"

Mrs. Broome leaned closer. "Across a ladder between your houses?"

"Yes. How did you know?"

"Hank noticed the ladder after he found Mr. Johnson on the floor in your front room."

A piece of potato went down the wrong way, and Miranda coughed. "What? What happened? He was fine when we left."

"Then he didn't hurt you?"

"Why would he do that?"

"That's just it. No one knows. He's had a stroke, and he can't tell anyone anything."

A stroke! After she and Lucy left? "But why would anyone think he'd hurt us?"

"The front door was kicked in. Hank suspected he'd forced his way into the house. Then there was no sign of you or Lucy."

"No. No. That wasn't it at all. Mr. Johnson helped me flag down a rescue boat."

She thought back to Sunday. Not only had Mr. Johnson perspired profusely, but he had gotten quite red in the face when he helped move things upstairs. That might have had something to do with the stroke, but it didn't explain the front door being kicked in. When she and Lucy left in the boat, he and the house were both fine.

"Mr. Slatterman was there! He was one of the rescuers! Didn't he tell anyone he'd seen us?"

"I asked Mrs. Slatterman about him yesterday when she came in to get groceries for her refugees. I don't think he's been back home since he left to help with the rescues."

Mrs. Slatterman's refugees. Then Dolores did have a houseful. "How did Hank get back to Osage? He couldn't have driven there. The water was too high."

"Father Donovan said–"

"Father Donovan?" The story was getting more and more confusing.

"He stayed a night here at the rectory after he left St. Mary's. That's how I know all this."

Miranda nodded. "Mr. Johnson told me Father went to the hospital to give Henry–" She stopped eating, and her whole body tensed. This could be the moment she found out. "Is Henry...? Do you know?"

"Father said he's still fighting."

"When was that? What night was Father at the rectory?"

Mrs. Broome pressed her lips together and looked off. "All the days are running together," she said, and then after a moment remembered. "Monday. Hank went back to Osage that morning – in a boat the Sisters rounded up for him – and he brought Mr. Johnson to the hospital. Father said Hank was hopping mad."

Two days ago. She worried how much fight Henry had left. "Why did Hank go home in the first place?"

"Peachie heard about the evacuation of the West End, and he had to tell her that, the last time he talked to you, you and Lucy were still at the house. She's barely holding it together, and she insisted Hank make sure you and Lucy were okay."

"So," Miranda said, "when he got back to the hospital, he had to tell her about Mr. Johnson and the front door being kicked in. And that Lucy was gone." Oh, no. Poor Peachie.

"You can imagine how she took it. With Henry so bad, and Lucy missing, she's absolutely beside herself." A broad smile

139

broke through the gloom on Mrs. Broome's face. "We can let her know Lucy is okay!"

"Yes! Of course! Are the telephones working?"

"We can call around the Highlands, but most of the other exchanges are flooded, so we can't call out. Actually, I'm not sure how we're going to reach her." Her smile faded.

Miranda set her fork down on the empty plate. The cold milk and hot food were doing their work, and her brain felt capable of concentrating again.

So the telephones wouldn't be of any use. And the mail, even if it got through, would take too long. There *had* to be a way to let Peachie know. As soon as possible.

~ ~ ~

"Excuse me. Excuse me." She wove through the stream of people strolling casually down the sidewalk, turning sideways when necessary and holding Lucy and the paper sack she and Mrs. Broome had hurriedly filled with donated clothing tight against her. A middle-age woman, absorbed in searching the faces of the pedestrians across the busy street, nearly collided with Miranda, forcing her to dive to the soggy patch of ground between the sidewalk and the road.

She had to get to Dolores's, and she had to make a decision about what to do about Peachie. Especially if she was going to do it today.

Lucy's head dropped to her shoulder. The rest of her small body soon sagged as well, doubling the weight in Miranda's arms. By the time they turned onto Dolores's street, her muscles pleaded for relief.

Hoping she'd remembered correctly the house number Mr. Slatterman gave her, she searched the facades of the houses and spotted the octagonal tower room before she saw the address. Slatterman's delivery truck was parked at the curb.

She carried Lucy up the concrete steps to the raised lawn and walked down the sidewalk that divided the front yard.

Painted stairs led up to a generous veranda, too elegant to call a porch.

The double entry doors, a dark oak, also suited the Victorian home. She knocked tentatively. Timmy, the Slattermans' youngest, must have been close by, because he answered immediately.

"It's Mrs. Kinley!" he called back into the house, his boyish voice so like Henry's that Miranda winced.

He ran off and left the front door hanging open. She stepped into the entry hall, so large it had its own fireplace, and closed the door behind her. The house was pleasantly warm, and a heartening whiff of vegetable soup and coffee drifted her way.

"Miranda?" Mrs. Slatterman burst out of one of several rooms off the hallway. "Ain't you a sight for sore eyes!" She moved nimbly across the polished wood floor, took Lucy from Miranda's arms, and settled her across her generous bust. "So you *did* manage to escape the likes of that no-good Mr. Johnson," she said, as softly as her gruff voice allowed. "You look positively done in, and this poor baby sound asleep!"

"I... We..."

"Let's take her upstairs. She can nap on my bed."

They started up the open stairway on the left side of the hall. Halfway up, Miranda peeked down into the front room, though maybe Dolores called it a parlor. Strangers in ill-fitting clothing reclined in tasteful chairs arranged around a flaming fireplace. A teenage girl had her head bent to a book, a little boy sat on the floor with a puzzle, and the adults talked in low tones.

Mrs. Slatterman carried Lucy through the first door off the upstairs hallway and placed her gently on a double bed. She opened the closet next to an unlit fireplace and pulled down a basket-weave blanket from the shelf. After slipping off Lucy's hat and shoes, she drew the blanket across the bed and tucked its satin-bound edges around her.

"Would you like a lie-down yourself?" she asked Miranda. "Or do you need something to eat? I've seen better color on a head of cauliflower."

Miranda set the paper sack on the floor next to a chifforobe. It wouldn't hurt to rest. She couldn't do anything or go anywhere until Lucy woke. "We just ate, but maybe I will lie down a few minutes." She studied Lucy's curls to avoid Mrs. Slatterman's eyes. One sympathetic look, and she'd be in tears. "I guess Mrs. Broome told you about Henry... about Father giving him Last Rites?"

"Yes. Yes, I know. But don't go thinking about that right now." Mrs. Slatterman made for the bedroom door. "Come down when you're rested, and we'll talk. Right now I need to make sure Ruth Anne ain't taken her eye off the soda bread that's baking for lunch. The girl sneaked off this morning to get a break from all the work, and I don't half blame her." The door closed behind Mrs. Slatterman without a squeak.

The bedroom was an oasis of aloneness and calm, the first she'd found since she left home on Sunday. She inhaled the silence and let it settle down in her.

If she could rest a bit, away from everything, she might be able to clear her mind and come up with a plan to get hold of Peachie. If she couldn't, and if Mrs. Slatterman didn't know a way, there was only one thing left to do. Go to the hospital.

She untied the oxfords she'd put on that morning, her only footwear now that her rain boots had floated off in the suitcase. Slipping under the basket-weave blanket, she nestled into a pillow covered by the satin bedspread and pulled the blanket up to her neck – the softest wool she'd ever put against her skin.

The bed felt especially luxurious after sleeping on an army cot for three nights with Lucy pressed up to her. She stretched out, stared at the smooth ceiling, and considered what to do next.

If she had to go to the hospital, should she take Lucy? Mrs. Slatterman would take good care of her here at Dolores's, but it seemed she was already so busy. And would that even help Peachie, only hearing Lucy was fine? No. She knew Peachie, and Peachie would need to see Lucy for herself.

She could ask Junior, assuming he was around, to drive them back to the flooded creek. They couldn't take the pontoon bridge since the foot traffic moved in only one direction – toward the East End – but she did have enough grocery money in her change purse to pay a boatman to take her and Lucy across the creek. Surely, one of them would be understanding of her plight and... and...

She woke with a start and glanced at the clock on the nightstand. Five after one. Her sudden movement woke Lucy.

~~~

The kitchen, it became apparent, was the Slatterman family's domain, and the refugees stayed confined to the parlor and the dining room. Junior played a game of checkers with Timmy at one end of a trestle table in the middle of the room, while the other two boys shared a large piece of paper and bickered, not quite loud enough to annoy their mother, over a drawing they'd made of an elaborate maze. Ruth Anne dried the lunch dishes, and Dolores put them away.

Dolores's slim frame and long hair, as dark and glossy as a drape of rich brown silk, made Miranda wonder what a twenty-two-year-old Mrs. Slatterman had looked like. Hard to imagine, watching the robust arms chop onions at the table next to the checker game then throw them into a huge pot of beans on the back of the gas range.

"Almost done here," she said, "then I'm putting my feet up and resting my aching back while you tell me everything."

Lucy skipped over to Timmy and watched him slide a red checker across the game board.

"How many refugees are staying with you?" Miranda asked.

"Seven," said Dolores. "We took in two small families on Sunday. Ruth Anne moved in with Mother since Daddy isn't

143

here, and we moved the boys down into the back bedroom so we'd have two bedrooms upstairs for the refugees."

"They're quiet enough," said Mrs. Slatterman, "but they act like paying guests, which they ain't. We could sure use Dolores's maid right now. I wonder if she got sent out of town. The good Lord only knows where the rescue workers are toting everybody off to."

"Mr. Slatterman was one of the men in the boat that came for me and Lucy," said Miranda.

"You don't say," said Mrs. Slatterman, a flicker of pride in her eyes. She settled into one of the kitchen chairs and, good to her word, lifted her stout legs and put her feet up in another chair, her ankles as trim as they must have been the day she married. "He stayed here one night and was gone the next day. Said he could do more good helping out somewheres than sitting around. Knowing that man, we won't see him again till the river gets itself back in its banks."

She took off her glasses and cleaned them with the hem of her plain black dress, the slick fabric worn to a shine. "I'm dying to hear how you outsmarted Mr. Johnson, but first," her voice dropped off, "tell me easy just how bad the store is."

Was there an easy way?

"On Sunday," Miranda started, "by the time it got dark, the water was up to the porches on most of the houses, and it had climbed St. Benedict's front steps. The church is completely underwater–

"And our store too," interjected Mrs. Slatterman. Her bosom lifted and fell as she sighed deeply.

"A good part of it, I'm afraid."

Mrs. Slatterman rested her glasses in her generous lap. Closing her eyelids, she slowly rubbed her temples. "Well," she said, finally looking up, "it would bother me a whole lot worse if everybody wasn't in the same boat."

No one smiled, nor did the boys snicker, at the unfortunate pun. The children's eyes had all turned anxiously upon their mother.

"But the upstairs is okay? All our stuff?" asked Ruth Anne, twisting the tea towel in her hands.

"It was when I left."

Miranda felt it might be a good time to tell them how much help Mr. Johnson had been on Sunday. She couldn't let everyone go on thinking he'd done something wrong.

"Hank don't know all that," said Mrs. Slatterman, her tone ominous. "He's thinking the worst, and I bet he'd as soon do that man in as look at him. Mr. Johnson better talk quick when he comes to."

Miranda hadn't thought about that. Not only did she need to let Peachie know Lucy was fine, but she had to set Hank straight before things got out of hand.

She told them next about everything that happened after they left Mr. Johnson – the boat ride, the truck ride, and how they ended up at the Madrid.

"The Madrid?" Ruth Anne squealed, her mood taking a sudden turn. "As soon as I'm twenty-one, I plan to get all dressed up and go dancing at the Madrid."

"You ain't stepping foot in that nightclub till you're married," said her mother, and turned back to Miranda. "What about Ben? Where's he been all this time?"

When Miranda told her he never made it home, the older woman's frown nearly caused her eyebrows to join in the middle. But after hearing how quickly the streets had filled with water Sunday morning, she nodded.

"I can't imagine but he's fine. Just couldn't get through."

"That's pretty much what Mr. Slatterman said." Though it wasn't any easier to believe now than it had been then.

"I heard," said Mrs. Slatterman, "the city has set up some kind of missing persons bureau at the Highlands Library. Maybe you could find out something there."

There was nothing Miranda would rather do, if she only had the time. Before she could voice that, Mrs. Slatterman went on.

"It's right upsetting, Henry getting Last Rites and all. Anything happens to him, it'll do me in. More than the flood ruining the store."

Miranda fought down her own sadness. "I'm worried about Peachie too," she said. "I have to get hold of her and let her know Lucy is fine. Can you think of a way besides the telephone? Mrs. Broome said you can't call out of the Highlands."

The wrinkles around Mrs. Slatterman's pursed lips drew closer together. "I reckon the police might help if they didn't have so much else to do right now. In the old days, people would send a messenger."

"I'll go," said Junior. He had returned to his checkers game but obviously hadn't missed a word. "I bet I wouldn't have any trouble making it to the hospital."

"I'd better go myself," said Miranda.

"Good night!" said Mrs. Slatterman, her chair groaning as she shifted her weight. "You're leaving? I thought you came to stay."

"I wish I could. But Peachie has to be in a terrible state over Henry, and if she can't talk to Lucy on the telephone, she won't be satisfied until she sees her. No telling what she imagines has gone wrong, after hearing about the busted front door and Mr. Johnson."

"You'll stay the night though?"

"No. We'll leave in a few minutes. You don't really have room for us, and Lucy looks rested." Lucy had lost interest in the checkers game and appeared ready to be on to something else.

"What about washing up first? You been sleeping in those clothes?"

Miranda put a hand to her hair, rough and stiff from needing a wash, and looked down at her disheveled dress. She'd changed Lucy's once in the last three days and her own not at all. The water spots from washing under her arms were hidden under her cardigan. "I'll change us both real quick. We only have a few more hours of daylight."

"How are you going to get to the hospital?"

"If you have any gasoline left in the truck, I could use Junior's help."

~~~

She'd seen Junior leave the grocery store in the delivery truck enough times to know he drove like Hank. The traffic on Bardstown Road crept slowly in both directions though and gave him no opportunities to pass. She leaned back in the bench seat and rested her hand on Lucy's knee.

The paper bag had felt heavier when she'd carried it out of Dolores's house. She thought of it again as they neared Baxter Avenue and unfolded the crumpled top. Inside, a smaller sack lay on her and Lucy's clothes. Inside that were three ham sandwiches wrapped in waxed paper, with two red apples weighing down the bottom. *Oh.* Mrs. Slatterman hadn't given her a chance to say thank you.

When Junior drove past the two cemeteries, she kept her eyes straight ahead and her mind on Peachie. If she could keep picturing Peachie's delight at seeing Lucy, she wouldn't have time to be terrified about Henry or relive the last day she'd spent at St. Mary's with her mother.

The closer Junior got to the flooding, the more often the heavy traffic came to a complete stop. They were never going to reach the hospital before dark.

"Let us out here," she said to him. "I can get there faster walking."

"You sure? Mother told me not to leave until you found a way across the creek."

"We'll be fine. Really. Tell her I insisted." They *had* to be fine. "Turn left here," she said as they reached Payne Street. "You can drop us off and go around the block to get back home."

The naps at Dolores's had done her and Lucy a lot of good, and they easily made the walk downhill to the floodwater. Sunshine slanted across the water, giving her the courage to maneuver Lucy around the groups of people standing near its edge and wait for the next boat to land.

A man rowed up alone in a long, empty skiff. He stepped into the floodwater in his black rubber boots and pulled the boat onto the cobbled street. A soldier standing next to a pick-up truck waved him down. The two men carried crates of cabbages to the skiff and stacked them between the seats. Miranda squared her shoulders and approached them.

"Excuse me," she said to the boatman. "Can you make room to take us across the creek? I'd be glad to pay you."

"Do you have a pass?" interrupted the soldier.

"A what?"

"A military pass. You can't go back into the central area without one."

His words sank in. Maybe she shouldn't have sent Junior back to Dolores's. No. She wasn't going to stop now. There had to be a way. "Can I get a pass?"

"That's not my decision. You'll have to go to Headquarters and see if they'll give you one."

"How far is it?" she asked, dreading his answer.

"There." He pointed up the hill. "On the left before you get to Hull Street. At Louisville Drying Machine."

She let out a breath, thanked him, and walked Lucy up the sidewalk.

The two-story brick building at the end of the block boasted a stately main entrance with the company's name carved in stone at the top. A well-groomed soldier stood guard at the front door, his lace-up leather boots nearly reaching his flared breeches and a matching brown belt fastened around his olive coat. He removed his hat, nodding politely, and opened one of the main doors.

She stepped into a reception area. Plain wooden chairs lined one wall, filled with men hunched forward, hats in hand, or leaned back, hats balanced on one knee, while everyone waited to see someone in charge. Since all of the military personnel seemed to have disappeared into the offices the Army had appropriated for their work space, she took a seat also.

After a few minutes, a door with a frosted glass panel opened, and an officer walked out, a powerfully-built man with a drawn face and tired eyes. "Who's next?"

The men on the chairs glanced at each other. One stood and followed the officer. The man was in and out quickly, and she dared hope there'd be enough daylight left for the rest of her and Lucy's journey. Several ahead of her took longer than expected though and, since none of the soldiers moving between the offices offered to help, it was over an hour before her turn came. She and Lucy had eaten every bit of the food Mrs. Slatterman fixed.

"How can I help you?" the officer asked, as she sat opposite him at his desk and put an arm around Lucy.

She explained to him quickly how she needed to get Lucy to her mother, who was at St. Mary's with Lucy's brother and frantic because she didn't know—

He held up a hand and stopped her. Sitting back with a sigh, he spoke with a finality that wasn't unkind. "There are hundreds, if not thousands, of citizens who don't know where their husbands and wives and children are. It's better if you stay in the East End where the child will be safe until she can be reunited with her mother."

She started to speak again and then, knowing he had the last word and that nothing she said at this point would sway him, rose to leave. If only there was something she could do so Peachie wouldn't have to wait and worry and imagine the worst about Lucy.

"I'm not asking for myself, you know." Her voice swelled with a mix of frustration and pleading.

The door opened behind her. The officer pushed back his chair, stood smartly, and saluted, but she didn't stop.

"My own husband has been missing for days. I'm not asking you to let me find him. I'm asking you to let me take my friend's daughter to her. Her son is dying, and she thinks something terrible has happened to her daughter. It's not as if I'm going to traipse all over the city. I just want to go to the hospital and let her see for herself that her daughter is fine."

The officer looked behind her instead of answering. "Colonel Stites. Sir."

"At ease, Lieutenant. What is it that you need, ma'am?"

She turned around to a man well decorated in silver eagles and medals. "I was hoping to get one of the boats to take us back downtown. We've been at the Madrid since Sunday and came over the pontoon bridge this morning. But then I found out something happened back home. Something that makes my friend think her daughter is in terrible danger. If I could have a pass to cross the creek so we can get to St. Mary's, I could let her see she's fine."

The colonel searched her face a long moment before he looked down at Lucy. "Here's a better idea." He nodded to the lieutenant. "Have one of your men commandeer a boat and see that these ladies are taken straight to the hospital."

~~~

The top half of a mailbox jutted out of the water on Magnolia. At the next corner, the boat turned north onto 12th Street. A policeman, standing on the steps behind the locked iron gates at Sts. Mary and Elizabeth's main entrance, waved them toward the driveway entrance.

The hospital grounds rose above the rest of the neighborhood. Nearby homes were partially immersed, but every floor of St. Mary's remained high and dry.

Mrs. Slatterman had grown up in the Cabbage Patch neighborhood the hospital was a part of, and she'd told Miranda the Sisters once raised their own cows and chickens. The pasture was sold when the Sisters needed the money to enlarge the hospital, and now St. Mary's sat disagreeably close to noisy, sooty railroad lines and manufacturing plants.

Behind the smoke stacks and water tower off to Miranda's left, a mackerel sky blended into a golden sunset. They'd made it before dark, but barely. The boatman steered up the brick driveway and killed the motor before they reached the end of the floodwater. She found the resulting quiet in the abandoned neighborhood unexpected and pleasing.

But she didn't like the look of Lucy's bluish lips, or that her small body shuddered from the cold. Two other policemen guarding the hospital ran up to brace the boat while the soldier sent along to assist her and Lucy carried them to a dry section of brick pavers. Miranda smoothed her coat and took a moment to steady her legs.

She thanked the soldier, and then the policeman who opened the door at the hospital's driveway entrance. Her hand tensed around Lucy's. As much as she wanted to take her to Peachie, she trembled at the thought of coming back to the place where her mother had died and Henry might do the same.

What appeared to be a receiving committee of doctors and nurses waited inside the door. One of the nursing Sisters, in a habit of all white, approached them and asked whether they'd come to seek medical help or escape the flood. The Sister's welcoming smile contrasted oddly with the worry in her eyes.

"Neither, really," said Miranda, saying a quick prayer they'd be allowed to stay. "My friend is here with her son who's gravely ill. I've brought her daughter to her." *Would* Peachie still be there? If something had happened to Henry... "It's a long story, but it's very important my friend sees that her daughter is okay."

"Are you planning to leave the child here?"

"If that's all right."

"And are you staying?"

"I've nowhere else to go."

"We'll put you down as refugees then. Come sit with me and give me your names."

After Miranda had satisfied her with the needed information and assured her they didn't require typhoid inoculations, the kindly Sister of Charity wiggled a finger beneath her starched wimple and kneaded a spot beside her deep-set eyes.

"We're begging cots at the moment. Maybe it would be best if you found your friend first."

Miranda pulled Lucy closer and glanced around the busy room. No one looked as if they had time to find Peachie for her. "How can I, since children aren't allowed on the hospital floors?"

"The rules are quite relaxed at the moment. We have no way around it with all the refugees here. Take the elevator up to the main entrance and find out what room or ward your friend's son is assigned to. After you've found him, come back and let me know. We may be able to set up cots for you in the corridor outside his room."

~~~

She found a set of stairs outside the receiving room. Lucy climbed them easily enough, but her own strength flagged on the way up. When they reached the main floor, the corridor was crowded, and several refugees had to move out of the way to let them pass.

The hospital couldn't have been more different from the last days she'd spent there with her mother. On those melancholy afternoons, the only sounds in the long, hushed corridors were the rustle of the Sisters' long skirts and the soft patter of leather soles against the hardwood floors.

Now, cots lined each side of the corridor as it stretched into the building. People tried to keep their voices low and their children close, but the previous calm had turned into a hubbub.

The atmosphere was cheerful though, as the Sisters and refugees attempted to lift each other's spirits. And the aroma of an appetizing supper, carted in by smiling student nurses, masked the Lysol that disinfected the toilet rooms and baths.

Miranda smiled at one of the children. For the most part, she kept her eyes forward, ignoring the commotion on each side of her and seeking to reach the end of the corridor as quickly as possible. A soft bell chimed twice like the call bell systems in the department stores, and she looked up, wondering which of the doctors or Sisters it summoned.

Somehow, the hospital had electricity, and the corridor was lit as well as warm. She hadn't seen an electric light on in the city since Sunday and couldn't imagine how the Sisters had managed it.

They came to a wide intersecting hall. Down on the right, *Sts. Mary and Elizabeth Hospital* was embossed on the colored glass arched over the hospital's front door. Her head cleared as she got a sense of where she was. The nagging feeling of being closed-in and half-lost subsided, and she led Lucy to the reception area near the front entrance.

"Excuse me," she said to a young woman whose bangs curled high on her forehead.

"Yes?" The receptionist's smile widened.

"Can you tell me what room Henry Ryan is in?"

"Patient or refugee?"

"Patient. A child."

The young woman reached for a slim stack of papers held together by a paperclip and flipped toward the back. "Ryan." She ran a finger down a list of names typed on the page, and then stopped.

"I'm not finding anyone named Ryan. Let me check the refugee list in case it was accidentally entered there." She reached for another set of papers and perused them. "Hmm. Not here either."

Miranda's heart thumped hard and fast, and her face flushed so hot she was afraid she'd pass out. She untied her scarf and shoved it in her coat pocket, unable to form the question that had to be in the young woman's mind also.

"Oh, wait! I bet I know what happened." The girl went back to the patient list. "Yes, here it is. Someone listed the last name as Henry."

"Then he's still here? Still..."

"Yes," said the young woman, her voice softening. "We lost two yesterday, but he's not one of them." She checked the list again. "Room 148." Her eyes lifted, and her smile returned. "Around the corner to the right and not far down on your left."

~~~

Miranda scanned the room numbers on the doors. Her heart insisted on racing, but she ignored it and kept searching. When she found 148, the door was shut. She knocked gently. No one answered. She inched the door open and peeked in.

The shade was pulled at the window, and it took a minute of staring into the dimness to see that the iron beds in the room held two small boys. Henry was in the bed on the left, his hair dark against the white pillow. He wasn't swallowed up in an oxygen tent as she'd feared, but an oxygen tank did occupy a corner of the room. He lay still without moving. She could barely breathe.

Cots flanked the side of each boy's bed. The cot next to Henry was empty. A woman, presumably the second boy's mother, turned over in her cot and sat up groggily.

"Can I help you?"

"I'm sorry to disturb you," Miranda choked out in what she had intended to be a hushed voice. "I was hoping to find Peachie. Is Henry... okay?"

"He's much better. Both of the boys are." She pushed up slowly from the cot and reached across her son's bed to straighten his covers.

"You just missed Peachie, but I doubt she'll be gone long. She hasn't hardly left Henry's side all week. Scared to, I think. Ever' time it looked real bad, she sung him a pretty song till he got some better. Heart-wrenching, it was. He pulled out of it last night, and she had a hard time believing it till this afternoon. That's when she decided to go to the chapel and say her thanks. I had to remind her she'd need a hat, and she borrowed mine."

The woman moved to the foot of the bed. "You can wait here if you'd like. Hank and my Stan took off for the men's refectory when they heard the Sisters were serving steak for supper. Mostly for the police from Virginia guarding the hospital, I think, but the Sisters don't mind. There's been no shortage of food, I have to say.

"I think we *will* wait here." Miranda remembered from her mother's time at the hospital that the chapel was on the third floor in the annex. A fairly long walk, with more sets of stairs, and they might end up missing Peachie anyway.

"Have you had supper?" the woman asked. "The boys had theirs before they fell back to sleep, and I'm going to go when Stan gets back."

"We haven't, but we'll wait for Peachie." Miranda took off Lucy's hat, got her comfortable in one of the wooden chairs in the room, and put their bag of clothes underneath. "Mommy will be here in just a few minutes," she whispered in her ear.

Lucy, uneasy since she first saw Henry, brightened. She nodded, her curls bouncing.

The woman looked at her more closely. "That has to be Lucy. She's the spitting image of her mother. Peachie's not going to believe her good luck. She didn't talk about it much, but I expect she thought her whole life was being stole from her. Something going on about a neighbor."

"Yes, but it was all a misunderstanding." Miranda crept closer to Henry. It was good to see his sweet face, even if it did look wan and drawn. Her hand moved to brush the straight strands of dark hair from his damp forehead. Afraid she'd wake him, she changed her mind.

"He's a little fighter, Henry is," the woman said. "The doctor said it's all good from here."

Miranda couldn't resist stroking the small, limp hand resting outside the blanket. Had it been only a week since Henry wanted so badly to be a boxer? Well, he got to have his fight after all. A good fight. And Peachie had been at his side, cheering him on.

~~~

Miranda couldn't stay put in the spare wooden chair. They'd come too far, and Peachie had been through too much, to wait any longer. She told the boy's mother she'd changed her mind about going to the chapel and walked Lucy to the back of the original hospital and into the annex.

The wood floor changed to linoleum, dark red and white squares. She happened upon the stairway then lost her sense of direction completely when they reached the third floor. A patient, shuffling past in his house shoes, led them to the chapel.

The tall entry doors, distinctly different from the rest, loomed over her and Lucy. She pulled out her scarf and threw it over her hair, realizing, as she tied it under her chin, how nervousness and excitement felt very much the same.

The carved doors had matching wrought-iron handles. She gave one a tug, and they slipped inside. The door sealed closed behind them, leaving the busyness and noise of the hospital out in the corridor.

Despite the suppertime hour, the two long rows of narrow pews teemed with kneeling refugees. Down in front, she could see a couple of the white bonnets the Sisters wore. Most of the Sisters, with the extra workload, likely prayed as they worked.

She ushered Lucy into a pew in the back then rose up on her toes to figure out which, if any, of the women in front of them was Peachie. The hat Peachie wore might not be her own, but there would be no mistaking her red curls.

Miranda spotted her in the first row, nearer the altar than even the Sisters. So close, she thought, a bit breathless, and yet all that way up front. Maybe it would be better to let Peachie finish praying first. She dropped to the kneeler.

The chapel was lit by candelabra hung on the side walls. Two more of the lights rested in the arms of matching angels, one on each side of the front altar. The entire altar area was framed in white wood, delicately carved, that rose to a peak crowned by a gold cross. A sky blue ceiling soared above the cross.

She silently voiced her own thanks for Henry's recovery then said a long and earnest prayer for Ben. Calm poured over her, easing her nerves and giving her strength. She enjoyed the moment's peace.

Peachie stood, her red hair suddenly visible above the others. Miranda's stomach jumped, and she leaned into the aisle for a better view. Her face broke into a grin as she watched her friend steal gracefully up the aisle.

Peachie's bent head lifted, and their eyes met. Her "Oh!" resounded through the chapel. She burst into a run. Heads turned as she tore past.

"Mommy!" Lucy scrambled across the seat and into the aisle.

Miranda joined her. Peachie wrapped her slender arms around the two of them and squeezed them close.

"You're okay. You're both okay." She leaned back, her eyes glistening. "Did you hear about Henry? Do you know he's getting well?"

Miranda nodded.

Peachie gave them another hug. Then she grabbed their hands and dragged them out of the chapel. Someone was clapping.

~~~

Peachie lifted Lucy into her arms. "Have you had supper?" she asked with a tender smile.

Lucy shook her head.

"Then let's get some!" She carried her to the stairway, Miranda at their side. "We'll go to the nurses' dining room. It's the next floor down. The Sisters are using every room they have to feed and bunk everyone. People are sleeping in the parlor, and I heard some of the Sisters gave up their own beds."

The dining room was a bright and pleasant space. Miranda reveled in the aromas that rose from the baked and simmered foods and floated across the air. She'd been afraid to return to the hospital, and it hadn't been easy, but there wasn't much better than having supper with Peachie.

A sign near the serving line indicated that the meal choices were cream of mushroom soup with cheesy corn muffins and strawberries, or chicken pot pie with mashed potatoes and yeast rolls.

"Where in the world are the strawberries coming from?" she asked Peachie.

"A produce dealer brought them to the hospital rather than let them spoil. There's been ice cream, and shrimp from some importer, though nothing much has sounded good until today."

"We should have come to the hospital sooner. Our meals haven't been nearly as fancy or generous."

Peachie's brow wrinkled, and Miranda added quickly, "Lucy always had enough."

They carried their trays to a small table in a corner for privacy. Miranda took off her coat and laid it across the back of her chair. Peachie pointed and giggled.

"*Where* did you get that dress?"

Miranda looked down at the dark brown cotton dress, the large silver buttons buttoned all the way up to the collar. The collar was pointed and large, as were the two pocket flaps just below it. She grimaced. Somebody's grandmother had last worn the dress.

"It's clean anyhow."

"But where..." A bubbly stream of giggles kept Peachie from saying more. She spooned part of her ample dinner onto an extra plate for Lucy.

"The refugee center at St. Francis of Assisi. From their pile of donated clothes. I was in a hurry, and it was the only one that looked as if it would fit."

"Tell me everything," said Peachie, squelching her laughter and sitting down. "Start with Mr. Johnson. Why did he break down your door?"

"He didn't as far as I know. He flagged down a rescue boat for us Sunday night, and Lucy and I left. The house was fine. Mr. Johnson was fine. I don't know what happened. He's here at the hospital, isn't he?"

"Yes. I've had to make Hank stay away from him. Mr. Johnson came to, but he's hard to understand. When the Ward Sister questioned him about what happened, he got all upset. She's not letting anyone near him." Peachie dipped her roll into the pot pie gravy. "What about Ben? Hank said the last time he talked to you, Ben was at work. He didn't make it home before you and Lucy left?"

"No. I thought he might be staying to do more rescue work, but I ran into a man who works with him, and he told me that, last he heard, Ben was on his way home. So now I have no idea where he is or what he's doing. It's hard not to worry."

"It'll be okay." A look of determination lit Peachie's eyes, and she smiled her engaging grin. "We'll all be back together soon. I can feel it."

Miranda returned her smile. Peachie had a knack for putting the bad stuff behind her and not letting it taint everything else. Maybe she should try that herself. "How has Hank been doing?" she asked. "He sounded terrible the times he called."

"You know Hank. He's no good at sitting still, and it's even worse when he's upset. It got to the point he couldn't stay in the room with Henry any amount of time. So he's been helping the Sisters. They think he's an angel sent from heaven, if you can believe that."

Miranda did find it hard to imagine, considering all the trouble Hank had given the Sisters in grade school. "What kind of things is he doing?"

"The bucket and barrel brigade, for one. Seagram's sent barrels of water over for drinking and cooking but, to get water for everything else, a group of men have been dipping buckets into the floodwater at the driveway, passing the buckets up a line to the hospital, and on up the fire escape to be used on the different floors.

"Then, after Hank got hold of the boat he brought Mr. Johnson to the hospital in, he started running his own little delivery service. Taking the doctors here and there, getting supplies, carrying messages to the telephone stations nearby that are still operating."

"No wonder the Sisters think he's heaven-sent."

"Especially Sister Mary Albert. I have a feeling she and Hank are two of a kind. Last Saturday, when the city started rationing water, the boilers weren't getting enough, and the heat wasn't on half the time. Refugees poured in all day, and it was everything the Sisters could do to find enough blankets to keep the patients and everyone else warm.

"Sister Mary Albert called to see if the L&N could ship tanks of water to the hospital. The tank cars came, but there was no way to get the water into the boilers. Saturday night, the water gave out, and we had no heat Sunday or Monday. Henry was so sick, and we were all so cold. That was the worst."

Miranda got an inkling of what it must have been like from the pain passing over Peachie's face.

"Hank said Sister Mary Albert left the hospital Monday morning determined to find a way to get heat. She and a companion managed to get through the flooding in an automobile driven by another man who's been helping them, but they were stopped on Fourth Street because the viaduct was flooded. You know – the one by Colorado Street?"

Miranda nodded.

"Sister got out of the automobile, climbed up the hill to the railroad track that goes over the viaduct, and hailed a K&I engine to take her out to the L&N shops. She hoped to get help pumping the water from the tanks to the boilers. When that didn't work out, the K&I engineer rode her to Standard Manufacturing. Right after Sister's visit, the company sent men to lay pipe from the tank cars to the boilers, and now the firemen from Sixth and Magnolia come whenever the water needs to be pumped. The hospital's been warm ever since, and the other Sisters can't stop talking about the spunk it took for Sister Mary Albert to do all that."

"It *is* pretty amazing." Miranda savored the last bites of her soup and muffin. "But what about the lights? How does the hospital have electricity when no one else does?"

"I'm not sure exactly. The Henry Vogt Company is generating it somehow."

Miranda might have told Peachie she was lucky, considering that much of the city had no heat or electricity and little food, but there was nothing lucky about what she'd been through. She told her instead about Mr. Slatterman in the rescue boat and about her and Lucy's days at the Madrid and how they crossed the pontoon bridge and saw Mrs. Broome at the church and the Slattermans at Dolores's. She left out anything that might distress her.

"And then you brought me Lucy, safe and sound. I should never have gotten so upset." Peachie reached over and laid her hand on Miranda's arm. "I can always depend on you."

Miranda struggled to take in Peachie's words.

"You didn't know that?"

"I never thought about it."

"From the very beginning. When my dad finally got mad enough and left for good. The times my mother went to the racetrack and left us kids to fend for ourselves. I always knew you'd be there for me. Just like now."

14

Thursday, January 28, 1937

Miranda slept well enough on the cot outside Henry's room, and breakfast with Peachie lightened her mood as always, but a heaviness crept into her spirit and a flutter unsettled her stomach as she made the walk upstairs to see Mr. Johnson. It would be upsetting to see him lying in a hospital bed, disabled and helpless.

She hoped that if she let him know she and Lucy were fine and Henry was on the mend, it might help him feel better. Hank, of course, wanted her to get to the bottom of what happened at the house.

"Sister?" She stopped the nun coming out of the men's ward. "I was wondering if I could speak to Mr. Johnson. I'm his next-door neighbor."

"He's sleeping at the moment. I could tell him you were asking about him, but it's best if he decides about company. We don't want anything to upset him."

"Is he better? Will he recover?"

"Many do," she said, her voice calm and reassuring. "His speech is already improving. You'll just need to be patient if you talk to him. Why don't you try back this afternoon around two?"

~~~

"His eyes lit up when I told him you were here at the hospital," the Ward Sister told her. "It will do him a world of good to see you. We have him out of bed and in a wheelchair. Why don't you take him down to the sunroom and get him to talk to you? The more he talks, the sooner he'll improve."

"He won't fall out, will he?" Miranda wasn't sure she wanted all this responsibility.

"We have him tied in. Don't worry. This will truly help his recovery. Wait here in the corridor, and I'll bring him out to you."

She returned with Mr. Johnson, freshly washed and shaved. A thick, cotton gown covered his barrel chest, and a soft blanket rested across his legs.

"Hello," said Miranda.

He dipped his head in greeting.

Sister gave her a nod of encouragement and turned the wheelchair so Miranda could take the handles.

She wheeled Mr. Johnson silently to the sunroom. She didn't expect him to talk along the way and preferred herself to wait till they were face-to-face. She hoped they could keep a conversation going as they had on Sunday and that they wouldn't revert to the days when he had influenza, their exchanges awkward.

Clouds scudded across the sky beyond the sunroom's multi-pane windows. A light rain which started that morning had stopped, and a brisk wind moved the gray clouds along.

She positioned Mr. Johnson by a window so he could see what was going on outside. The grounds in back were high enough above the street to be out of the flooding, and several policemen patrolled it. She also took a seat by the window and started with the good news.

"Henry is better," she said. "The doctor said he's on the mend."

One side of Mr. Johnson's mouth and mustache lifted in a smile. She cringed at his misshapen face and hurried to rein in her reaction before he noticed.

"Lucy is doing well also."

He didn't say anything, but he seemed pleased.

What next? "I heard the river crested yesterday. It started going down last night."

"Goo..ood," he replied. "Goo..ood."

A few words at last. Now what? She didn't want to ask him how he was, when it was obvious everything he did took great effort.

"Lucy and I ended up at the Madrid Sunday night. The nightclub downtown. We stayed until yesterday." She waited a moment then said her next words with as much kindness as possible. "Do you remember what happened Sunday after we left?"

He nodded slowly.

"Can you tell me?"

He nodded again. "I... I was... leaving. Fire... had gone... gone out. Heard a loud... loud noise... turned off... flashlight... carried a chair... down... downstairs...

"Looters. Mad. I... was mad. Cracked one... over the head... but they got... away."

His face, still discolored from his apparent fall, contorted with emotion. Tears dropped to his reddened cheeks.

"Stop! Please! You don't have to say anymore!"

He grabbed a fistful of the blanket, squeezing hard with his good hand.

"I'm so sorry," she said. "I didn't mean... Maybe you should lie down and rest now."

She rolled him back to the ward, her legs wobbling. Sister instructed two student nurses to put him to bed.

"I'm sorry," Miranda told her. "I'm afraid it didn't go very well."

"Not to worry," Sister said, her smile sympathetic. "You did more good than you realize."

15

Friday, January 29, 1937

Henry and Lucy were on his bed drawing, and Miranda and Peachie were playing gin rummy on the cot beside them — cards courtesy of Stan — when a student nurse poked her head in the room.

"Mrs. Kinley?"

"Yes. That's me," Miranda said.

"Sister wanted me to tell you that Mr. Johnson would like to speak with you. She said to come again at two, if that's all right."

Miranda glanced at Peachie, who knew she had no desire to revisit the day before.

"Okay. Tell her I'll be there."

She couldn't think what else Mr. Johnson would have to say, now that everyone knew about the looters. She didn't mind speaking with him. She just hoped he could talk without getting agitated. After a good night's rest, she was feeling less anxious about being at the hospital.

"Maybe he just needs some company," she said to Peachie.

Thankfully, she'd had a good lunch before she went up to the men's ward. It was hard to see Mr. Johnson in his feeble condition, and her knees tended to go weak.

He was in a wheelchair again, and they went down to the sunroom. The sky had cleared to a sparkling blue, and sunshine brightened the grounds outside the room's many windows.

"Thank... you... for coming."

"You're looking better today," she said, and gave him an encouraging smile.

"Would you... do... something? Please. Contact... my sister."

"Your sister?" She shook her head. That couldn't be true. "Didn't you tell Dr. Lathrop you had no family?"

His face twisted into a scrunched frown. Miranda tensed forward in her chair.

"Edda," he said.

"Edda is your *sister*?"

When he looked at her oddly, she realized she'd given herself away. She squirmed inside, knowing she'd have to explain.

"I have a confession to make. When Ben and I were taking care of you, I was looking for a piece of paper to leave a note and saw your photograph in the desk. I'm sorry, but I picked it up and looked at it and read the back. I thought you'd been married, and Edda was your wife." She put a hand to her face. Her hot cheek warmed her cold fingers.

"No." He slowly and painstakingly explained to her that he and Edda were on their way to visit their grandparents in Germany when the photograph was taken. Five years later, he was back in Europe, fighting in the war.

"Paintings... in front room."

"Are of Germany and Europe?" she asked.

"Black... Forest," he said, then told her he couldn't seem to paint them in the vivid colors he remembered from his first trip.

Miranda hadn't seen any indication in his house that he painted, and then she remembered the closed door.

"Edda lives...," he said, "in Jasper... Jasper, Indiana."

"You take that newspaper."

"Yes. To know... she's still alive."

Miranda had to think a moment. She realized he was reading the obituaries.

"You don't keep in touch?"

He didn't answer right away.

"I can't... hide... any longer."

"Hide?" Her stomach lurched, and her lunch threatened to come up. Surely, Mrs. Slatterman and Hank hadn't been right all this time.

Mr. Johnson struggled through the rest of the story. He'd been hanging wallpaper for a wealthy woman in Jasper. An expensive ring, a family heirloom for over a hundred years, went missing, and the housemaid told everyone she saw him going through the jewelry box in the woman's bedroom. It was the housemaid's word against his, and she'd been with the family for years.

Fool people should have kept the ring in a safe, he said. The family was irate, but he couldn't return something he didn't have, and he certainly didn't have the kind of money it would take to compensate them. They threatened to have him arrested.

During the war, Mr. Johnson told Miranda, he'd been imprisoned in Germany, and he couldn't endure the thought of being locked up again. He fled with his life savings before the sheriff could arrest him, and he changed his name. Maybe he wouldn't have been charged with the theft after so many years – ten, he said – but he'd been afraid to take the chance. Confined now by the stroke, he had nothing else to lose.

"I miss... Edda. Unfair to her... too. Left her... all alone. Our parents... gone."

Miranda shook all over by the time he finished the tragic story. Poor Mr. Johnson. Poor Edda. How could she help them?

"I'll send a telegram," she said. "As soon as I can. But I'll ask Edda to contact *me*. I won't say anything about you."

~ ~ ~

After supper, Hank brought a newspaper up from the men's refectory and gave it to Miranda to read. He'd found a paper for her the evening before also, but a lot of that news – the U.S. Troops, the out-of-state police, the pontoon bridge– she'd already experienced herself. There *had* been that one article about the deaths attributed to the flood. She'd rushed through it to see if any names were mentioned. There'd been no names, only the numbers of people and causes of death.

She took the Friday newspaper to her cot outside Henry's room. Sitting with her legs stretched out and her shoulder against the wall, she opened the newspaper gingerly. It consisted of more pages than the one she'd read at the Madrid, so it wasn't as flimsy, but the many hands that had held it that day had added numerous tears and folds.

Electric service was restored in the East End. Workmen had completed a connection between electrical lines near Lyndon and a high tension line from the Dix Dam. She stopped reading the article when her eye caught another title. "Refugee List," it said. Beginning in that issue, the newspaper would publish the names of refugees, their home address, and their current location.

Could Ben be on the list? She sat up, her feet itching to run to Peachie. But after flipping to the page where the list started, she decided to wait and see if she found him before she got everyone excited.

The list went on for pages. She guessed the newspaper had obtained the names from the missing person's bureau at the Highlands Library after the library received the information from the refugee centers. Her own name should be listed somewhere.

The names were grouped under the different centers. She skipped to the Madrid and ran her eye down the column. There it was. *Kinley, Miranda and one child, Osage.*

Maybe she really *could* find Ben. She'd have to go back and search all the shelters, assuming he'd gone to one. She still couldn't imagine what had happened that kept him from coming home.

She read slowly through the *K*s at each of the locations. When she found him – *Kinley, Benjamin, Osage* – an involuntary cry, so loud she surprised herself, flew from her mouth and garnered looks from the other people in the corridor.

She searched back up the page for the name of the refugee center where he was listed. *Crescent Hill Christian Church.* This time she noticed something printed below it. *Contagion Hospital.* She stared at the words, not wanting to believe them.

The boy at the Madrid, the one who'd had measles, was taken to a church in Crescent Hill the doctor had called a contagion hospital.

16

Saturday, Jan 30, 1937

The floodwater had receded a good distance from the hospital grounds. She and Hank debated whether they'd need the boat or could take his Ford to get her to the East End. The automobile would make it through the streets in the immediate area with no problem, but they couldn't be sure what they'd encounter on the way to the pontoon bridge.

They decided on the Ford for its warmth and comfort, figuring they could try different routes along the way if need be. In any case, they could always come back for the boat. Peachie hated to see her go, but she and Hank were as anxious as Miranda to find out if Ben was okay.

They started out after breakfast. She enjoyed the sense of liberation the drive away from St. Mary's gave her, though the scrambled eggs and milk she'd managed to get down gurgled at the thought of another hospital ahead. With Ben in it, and sick with what? Measles? Scarlet fever? Typhoid? She tried hard to hold back her worry until she found out the truth.

Whenever they came upon a flooded street, they judged the depth of the water by how far it lingered above a sidewalk or how high it covered a door. Hank chanced the streets the Ford could drive through without submerging the tailpipe, having to backtrack only once when a section was roped off because of a cave-in. A policeman advised them of the best place to cross Broadway, where the flooding had been the highest.

By the time they reached Jefferson Street, they were past the worst. Hank parked not far from the pontoon bridge. Groups of men and soldiers still congregated at the edge of the floodwater, not as close now to the foot of the bridge, but the area wasn't crowded as before.

A woman and boy approached the ramp. A soldier stopped them, his arms in constant motion as he talked. He pointed north, and they walked off in that direction.

"I wonder why he didn't let them cross," she said to Hank. "There are other people on the bridge."

"Only men," he said. "And look. Most of them are carrying boxes."

"Don't tell me I can't cross again."

"Hold on." Hank got out and spoke to the soldier.

"All good," he said, settling back in the driver's seat and pulling away. "There's a train shuttling back and forth every hour between the stockyards and Crescent Hill."

"Thank goodness." Pontoon bridge or train, she didn't care as long as she reached Ben.

Hank turned onto Wenzel. "Do you want out at Market Street? That's closest to the train tracks."

"No, take me to the main gates. There's a telegraph office Ben walks to sometimes after work to send his parents telegrams. Do you think it'll be open?"

"Hard to say. You want to send the Kinleys a telegram?"

"Yes, they have to be worried sick, and I told Mr. Johnson I'd send his sister one too."

Hank didn't say anything, and she guessed he hadn't quite let go of his opinions about Mr. Johnson.

A steady trickle of people made their way into the main entrance of the Bourbon Stockyards. She told Hank she'd be fine from there and promised to let him and Peachie know about Ben as soon as she could. She opened the passenger door, and the outside air carried in the lingering stench of cattle and pigs.

The telegraph office was open, and long lines trailed to the door. With so many people ahead of her, she'd probably miss the next shuttle. But she had promised Mr. Johnson, and she didn't know when she'd have the next opportunity.

The wait gave her time to think about what to say in the telegrams, and she hoped to have it figured out by the time she reached the clerk. How did she reassure the Kinleys Ben was fine when she didn't know herself? And what would she say to Edda without raising suspicion in the minds of the townspeople at the local telegraph office?

~~~

The passenger car Miranda boarded was nearly full when the shuttle train left the stockyards. An odd assortment of parcels occupied the overhead rack, and her paper bag didn't look at all out of place.

She leaned her head against the window as the train forded Beargrass Creek and crossed Spring Street, her mind still on the telegrams. Had she said the right things?

EVACUATED TO EAST END MORE LATER
MIRANDA

She'd purposely kept the Kinleys' message short. They'd probably think it peculiar she sent the telegram instead of Ben but, if it were her own children and she was worried about them, she'd rather receive *some* news than none at all.

It had taken longer to figure out Edda's telegram, and she'd changed the final word from *important* at the last minute.

PLEASE TELEPHONE WHEN LINES OPEN IN
LOUISVILLE SHAWNEE 2365J URGENT
MIRANDA KINLEY

She'd still have to be discreet when Edda called. People
were notorious for listening in on others' conversations, but
the telephone was faster than mail.

Oh well, she'd done the best she could. As she'd tried to do
for Lucy. Their evacuation might not have been the perfect
journey, carried out with a clear head and steady nerves, but
Lucy arrived safe and healthy at St. Mary's, and Miranda
couldn't ask for more than that.

The train rolled into Crescent Hill, with Frankfort Avenue
running alongside on the right. On the left, a large lawn led
back to a tall, red brick building with a white bell tower. It had
been a long time since she'd seen St. Joseph's Orphanage,
though Ben must pass it fairly often, working on the freight
trains.

The brakes beneath the passenger car squealed as the train
slowed and stopped at a side street. She followed the other
passengers down the steps, and then crossed Frankfort Avenue
to reach a sidewalk on the other side.

"Excuse me," she said to an older lady toting groceries in a
hand cart. "Do you know where the Crescent Hill Christian
Church is?"

"On Crescent Avenue," the lady answered, nodding back
across Frankfort Avenue to the side street where the train had
stopped. "A little ways up on the right."

Miranda thanked her and waited on the sidewalk as the
engineer aboard the switch engine backed up the train – a coal
car, three passenger cars, and the caboose – and returned to the
stockyards. She crossed the cleared tracks and walked up
Crescent Avenue. A residential street, it was more charming, no
doubt, when the trees were in bloom and the weather wasn't
cloudy and chilly.

Set amid the homes, a red-brick church came into view on her right. Tall, stained-glass windows rose high above arched, wooden doors, and an attractive girl in her early twenties stood on the sidewalk in front of the church steps.

Her dress and sweater looked as if they'd come from Byck's, the expensive ladies' store downtown, and she wore them with the poise only those accustomed to money could carry off. Miranda was relieved she had her own clean dress on under her coat and that she'd had the opportunity to wash her hair, even if it had been with floodwater from the bucket brigade. The girl held a cigarette to her lips and drew in deeply.

"Excuse me," said Miranda. "I'm looking for my husband, and I read in the newspaper that he was here at the church, in the contagion hospital. Do you happen to know where I can find him?"

The young woman turned her head and blew a stream of smoke through the air. "What's his name?"

"Ben Kinley."

"Oh, yes. Good thing you're here." She tapped ashes onto the sidewalk. "His fever broke a couple days ago, and we're having trouble keeping him in bed. He's wanted to go home and make sure you were okay."

"What's wrong with him? Will he be all right?"

"The policemen who brought him here from one of the canteens were concerned he had typhoid. It was only a case of influenza. He's been knocked out most of the week, but he'll be fine." The girl dropped her cigarette and ground it into the concrete with the toe of her leather pump. "Come on. I'll show you to his room."

Miranda followed her to a building attached to the back of the church, wishing they could walk faster. "Are you helping out here?" she asked. It was hard to guess, dressed as the girl was, exactly what she did.

"Yes. I'm a nurse. Though normally I work as a stewardess. The airline sent us to help out." She opened the door and held it for Miranda.

The building, which looked to house the Sunday school when it wasn't acting as a hospital, reeked with the sharpness of rubbing alcohol. All the doors in the hallway were shut, unlike St. Mary's where some had hung open. The girl stopped, knocking on one of the doors, and opened it a few inches.

"I'll leave you alone," she whispered, and then called into the room. "Okay to come in? You have company."

"Sure."

Miranda's breath caught at the sound of Ben's voice, and the last of her fear fell away. She slipped into the Sunday school room and closed the door behind her.

"Miranda!"

Her smile had to be as wide as the one she saw on his face.

"How the heck did you find me?" He sat against a pillow that cushioned his back from the metal rails at the head of the bed. The curtains at the windows were pulled open, and he'd been reading his pocket manual on steam engines.

She laughed, letting her bag of clothes fall to the floor, and rushed to his side. Ben dropped the manual and drew her into his arms. The answer to his question wound up muffled against his chest. She breathed in his warmth and let her body relax into his.

When he let her go, she straightened and took a long look at his face, resting her hand against his cheek. "I've missed you terribly."

Then she perched on the edge of his bed and told him everything that happened after he left. He let her talk, asking only a few questions, and seemed troubled by the boat ride in the rough current and rain.

After she described the harrowing trip across the pontoon bridge, his teasing tone assured her he was indeed better. "Wasn't that kind of drastic, just to get rid of my robe?"

Their laughter echoed through the large, empty room. It felt good to laugh with him, to laugh at all. She made light of the rest of the story, as much as she could, their moods sobering whenever they talked about Mr. Johnson.

"...and so Hank drove me to the stockyards and, after I sent Edda and your parents telegrams, I rode the shuttle here."

He pulled her close again, his breath on her neck. "You've been through a lot."

She hesitated to share her next thoughts, but she wanted to get things straight between them, once and for all. She sat up and steadied her voice.

"I saw the orphanage from the shuttle. As much as you go by there, you must have thought about wanting to adopt so many times."

His hazel eyes grew pensive. He looked down at her hands and took one in his. "You were right when you thought it would be tough to evacuate. That it would be hard on Lucy. So I trust you on this. If you say you're not ready, I'm good with that. If you never feel you can, that's okay too." Looking up, he squeezed her hand. "I'm sorry for leaving you and Lucy. I had no idea it would turn out like this."

She leaned closer and embraced him with her eyes. "It didn't turn out so badly."

17

Saturday, July 31, 1937

A warm breeze blew in the kitchen window and ruffled the dimity curtains. At the sink in front of the window, Miranda rinsed the blackberries Mr. Johnson had given her the evening before. She turned off the water, and voices drifted into the kitchen from his backyard.

"Do not overdo, Jupp. It will be a hot one today."

Miranda carried the colander of blackberries to the kitchen table, taking care not to drip on her new linoleum floor. Despite all the troubles brought on by the flood, a few good things had come from it.

Their neighborhood was quarantined the day after she found Ben, and they'd had to remain at the contagion hospital four more days. Ben was stronger by then anyhow, and he had needed that strength, once they reached the house, to repair the front door, clean out the mud in the basement, and nail down the buckled wood flooring on the first floor.

Unlike most of their neighbors, they were able to stay at the house while they worked. The potbelly stove supplied heat, once Ben got it vented permanently, and they ate the food that the boxes and cans she'd stored on the second floor provided.

After weeks spent cleaning the house bottom to top, they tackled Mr. Johnson's house, with Hank providing a good amount of help. Edda arrived the first of June and took on the finishing touches. She'd resigned from her teaching position at the end of the school year and sold her house in Jasper. She and Mr. Johnson thought about selling his house and living in Jasper, but he didn't want to go back. Edda didn't care. She was overjoyed to have her brother again.

He hoped to get on with his wallpapering business by the next year. With *Johnson* on both his work truck and the deed to his house, he decided it would be simpler to stick with that name.

The name of Josef Geist was cleared six months after Mr. Johnson fled Jasper. The authorities had distributed flyers to pawnbrokers in the area, and the housemaid was caught trying to sell the heirloom ring one Saturday in Evansville. Ten years wasted in loneliness and fear. At least Mr. Johnson had Edda now.

Miranda gathered flour and lard from the pantry and made dough for the crusts of her blackberry pies. She moved her mother's pitcher, aglow with orange and yellow zinnias, to one side of the kitchen table, rolled out the dough, and cut narrow strips for the lattice tops. When the pies were ready for the oven, she stood back and admired her handiwork.

Every time she'd made a pie since Christmas, she'd thought of the feast that covered Mr. Johnson's kitchen table. She never got up the nerve to ask him about all the food, but she mentioned it once to Edda.

"Oh, yes," Edda told her, in her slightly German accent. "At Christmas, Jupp always took treats to his customers for whom he hung paper. He did that many years in Jasper."

~ ~ ~

After the pies cooled, Miranda walked one of them down to the Slattermans. Enough rain had fallen since the river retreated to thoroughly wash the sidewalks clean of the mud that had covered the neighborhood.

The sun bounced off the shiny hood of Hank's sedan, blinding her for a second. Between the Sisters at St. Mary's not charging anyone who stayed at the hospital during the flood and Hank working overtime to salvage parts off the assembled Fords that had been underwater, he'd managed to make payments on his automobile despite the time off work.

Everyone had their hands full, but especially Mrs. Slatterman, trying to keep the grocery store running on top of taking care of Mr. Slatterman, who'd nearly died of exposure doing rescue work. He might never fully regain his health, Dr. Lathrop said, and Junior had taken over the early morning trips to the Haymarket.

On the bright side, Ruth Anne had graduated in her lovely white dress with the girls from Atherton High School, since Shawnee wouldn't reopen until the new school year. Mrs. Slatterman had decided in the spring that she wanted one of her children to go to college, and Ruth Anne was leaving in September for a state teachers' college.

The bell above the grocery store door jingled as Miranda walked in. She had yet to grow tired of the familiar neighborhood sound.

"What have you got there?" Mrs. Slatterman stopped emptying a case of applesauce and leaned her weight on the counter beside it.

"A pie. Mr. Johnson brought some blackberries over last night." Thankfully, she could mention Mr. Johnson's name these days and not get her head bitten off.

"Good of them to share. That Edda – if she ain't always generous and full of good advice. I enjoy talking to her every time she comes in."

Miranda slid the pie pan across the counter. "I thought Mr. Slatterman might enjoy this."

Mrs. Slatterman leaned down and took a whiff. "Smells tasty." She straightened and set two more jars of applesauce on the shelf. "You're not still worrying and thinking it's your fault he got sick? You ain't the only one he rescued, you know."

"I know, but I feel bad."

"No need. He ain't glad to be laid up, but he's glad he done it."

~~~

On her way home, Miranda stopped on the sidewalk to watch Ben and Hank play baseball with the younger boys in the neighborhood. Pepper, taken care of through the flood by a couple nearby who hadn't evacuated, had already been out to do his morning business. Everyone would be safe from his terrorizing till evening.

The ballgame took up three backyards, grassy and green and nothing like the summer before when the drought had nearly stripped the yards down to dirt. The flood revived the soil, but it had demolished the shanty between her house and Peachie's. The W.P.A. hauled the rubble away, leaving an empty lot, the makings of a ball field.

Henry, suntanned and strong, was playing first base. Timmy Slatterman covered second and third. Hank was up to bat, and Gil was pitching. A good little pitcher, Hank had told her, for a seven-year-old.

A ball cap sat cocked to the side of Gil's brown hair. He leaned back on one leg, drawing the ball behind him, then flung it toward the makeshift home plate. Ben was likely proud of Gil's pitching form, but she couldn't keep from thinking how dear he looked in the striped shirt and navy shorts she'd made him for summer.

He'd come home with them from the orphanage not long after Edda arrived. Most people adopted the littlest ones, and Miranda always thought she wanted a baby girl, but when they saw Gil, they knew, and Ben couldn't have been more pleased.

Gil wasn't so old yet that he didn't enjoy being tucked in and read to and kissed goodnight. Before long, he'd be running home from St. Benedict's to see what she'd fixed him for lunch.

And not long after, when it grew cold again, the three of them would take the train to spend Christmas with the Kinleys.

She wouldn't think beyond that, because there was no sense imagining life would be perfect. It helped, though, to be thankful for everything good.

Made in the USA
Lexington, KY
02 June 2019